NO SPECIAL

When Skinny, a mercenary cop, puts it to Tony Curbel that he can get him out of jail if he agrees to spy on his own family, Tony is faced with a wrenching decision. He knows his own innocence and the fact that he suspects his father of framing him spurs him to agree to Skinny's suggestion. Once free he investigates his family's affairs, leading to the discovery that their 'employment agency' isn't all that it seems: they buy children. The 'agency' gets rich taking children from Central America to menial jobs in the United States. But then Tony's father disappears, and only by digging up the past can Tony prevent his family from tearing itself apart.

NO SPECIAL HURRY

James Colbert

ATLANTIC LARGE PRINT

Chivers Press, Bath, England.
Curley Publishing, Inc.,
South Yarmouth, Mass., USA.

Library of Congress Cataloging-in-Publication Data

Colbert, James.
No special hurry / James Colbert.—Large print ed.
p. cm.—(Atlantic large print)
ISBN 0–7927–0265–4 (lg. print)
1. Large type books. I. Title.
[PS3553.O4385N6 1990]
813′.54—dc20
90–31594
CIP

British Library Cataloguing in Publication Data

Colbert, James
No special hurry.
I. Title
813.54 [F]

ISBN 0–7451–9818–X
ISBN 0–7451–9830–9 pbk

This Large Print edition is published by Chivers Press, England, and Curley Publishing, Inc, U.S.A. 1990

Published in the British Commonwealth by arrangement with Penguin Books Ltd, and in the U.S.A. and Canada with Houghton Mifflin Co.

U.K. Hardback ISBN 0 7451 9818 X
U.K. Softback ISBN 0 7451 9830 9
U.S.A. Softback ISBN 0 7927 0265 4

For V and for
Hector and Aida Trau

The world breaks everyone and afterward many are strong at the broken places. But those that will not break it kills. It kills the very good and the very gentle and the very brave impartially. If you are none of these you can be sure that it will kill you too but there will be no special hurry.

ERNEST HEMINGWAY
A Farewell to Arms

My special thanks to Gerard van der Leun and Tatiana Wilcke for their help in the past; and to John Sterling, Marie B. Morris, and Ronald C. Filson who, truly, have made all that follows possible.

CHAPTER ONE

For almost an hour I had watched as he worked on the crude, star-shaped design, etching it carefully with a sewing needle into the soft skin between his thumb and first finger. Now he sat on the corner of the metal-frame bunk, hunched over, intent in that rapt way only a seventeen-year-old can be intent, a bottle of ink clasped tightly between his knees, the marked hand draped over the edge of the rusting iron sink.

He dipped the needle into the ink and lifted it out, a shiny black drop quivering on its tip, and I asked, 'You know a tattoo will never come off?'

He smeared the ink into the design, then looked at me irritably, lips pursed, one eyebrow arched scornfully in a way that reminded me of myself at his age, when I had practiced bad-ass looks in the mirror, T-shirt sleeves rolled up, muscles flexing.

I added, 'It's going to hurt.'

He shook his head indulgently, then dipped back into the ink, smiling slightly as he did so.

'Everyone who sees it will know you've been in jail.'

His smile broadened, rounding his dull features, and without looking at me again, he set his shoulders in a preoccupied way and tossed his curly red-brown hair over one narrow shoulder.

His name was Randy. I had found him two nights before, wandering up and down the cellblock, newly admitted and not exactly certain why the tough guys, the ones with their solid bodies and their long, dull stares, were whistling at him and laughing as they invited him into their cells. So I had taken him in, reluctantly giving myself the role of his protector, and after a time I had explained to him that *white meat* was a term not always reserved for the breast of a chicken. And he had looked at me then just as he had looked at me a moment before, indulgently, half-amused, as if *I* were the one who needed help, and said, 'Give me a break Tony,' to which I had simply raised and dropped one shoulder in a resigned shrug meant to convey certain knowledge.

Now he added, 'You remind me of my mother.'

'Wait until it gets infected,' I warned.

'It's not going to get infected,' he replied sourly. 'I watched the guy yesterday, start to finish. He showed me what to do.'

'What guy?'

'The tattoo-guy. You know him.' Randy gestured behind his back, pointing with the needle.

I looked away, not bothering to observe

that his description fit half the men locked in with us, then asked over my shoulder, 'How much did he charge you?'

Randy did not reply right away but again dipped the needle into the ink and brought it out. As he held it close to his face and studied it, he answered absently, 'He charged five dollars for the needle, three for the ink. Eight dollars.'

My head jerked around involuntarily. By prison standards—for men who were paid ten cents an hour, *when* the prison could find them paid work—eight dollars was a considerable amount of money.

'At what interest?'

Randy smeared the ink, dipped into the bottle, smeared more ink.

'He didn't say anything about any interest.'

'He will,' I said.

'I won't pay it,' Randy replied with a teenager's smug, that-settles-that finality.

He will, I thought, and for a moment it was hard to look at his young face, *and you will.*

He was jabbing the needle now, going into his design too deeply, and blood was mixing with the ink, causing it to smear and to run along the weblike little creases in his skin.

I looked away and for a few minutes watched the cons moving idly back and forth, killing time on the strip, the ten-foot-wide floor that ran the length of the cellblock, from the door to the showers; cells on one side, steel wall on the other. A guard passed on the overhead walkway, whistling and tapping his stick on the steel rail. I looked up, following his progress without interest, imagining through the long, narrow windows behind him New Orleans's downtown, not a mile away: the secretaries in bright dresses on their way to work, the men in suits, the newsstand where I used to buy the morning paper. I pictured the newsman's hand, tough and callused, stained with newsprint; the cup of coffee I customarily drank standing up, glancing only briefly at the headlines before I turned to the commodities reports, the neat, orderly columns of numbers that prepared me for the day's work ahead.

For nine years I had managed one of my father's offices, advising wealthy Central American clients how they might maneuver around whatever currency restrictions prevailed at the time. Invariably those clients wanted to get their money out of their home country and into this one; it was my job to recommend that they convert their money into goods—timber, coffee, stamps, bananas, tin, anything that had intrinsic value—and then to arrange for those goods to be moved up here and sold. Since my fee was based upon the number of U.S. dollars my clients deposited after the sale of the goods, it seemed to be in my own best interest to stay abreast of the market trends. My interests seemed to coincide with those of my clients—although later I learned that most of my clients were representing my *father's* best interest, and the fees I had worked in good faith to earn were nothing more than money to keep me distracted.

I turned back to Randy and asked, 'How big a man is the tattoo-guy?'

'You know him,' Randy repeated. He dabbed at his hand with a folded tissue. 'He wears a bandanna all the time.'

It would be him, I thought, picturing the glassy-eyed biker who wore a bandanna because he chewed tobacco with his mouth open and occasionally liked to wipe at the brown spittle that drooled down his chin. A massive gut encircled him; his fat arms stuck out from his sides, a veritable showcase of tattoos.

'Pleasant fellow,' I observed drily.

'Not really,' Randy said.

The skin between his thumb and first finger was now smeared with ink and oozing blood and looked as if he had caught it in a closing steel door.

I turned away again, in time to see the tattooed biker approach our cell in that oddly tentative way prisoners go from one cell to the next. I knew he would not enter without permission from us both and simply glanced past him.

He called out, 'Hey, Randy, how's it

going?'

Randy looked over his shoulder, saw with relief who it was, and replied, 'Come on in. I think I have a problem.'

I know you have a problem, I thought, but the most immediate part of it was the mess he was making of his hand; so I pushed myself upright and stood outside the cell door, allowing, if he turned sideways, room for the biker to enter.

As he started to pass he smiled dimly, showing in the gap where his front teeth should have been a dark brown wad of tobacco.

I moved just slightly, but enough to block his way, and said, 'Eight dollars is too steep, pal.'

It took him a moment to comprehend that, and I could see it coming, the way he was working up to his hard-ass look, squinty-eyed and malevolent.

'What's it to you?' he asked.

'My money,' I replied.

That sank in slowly.

'You two married?' he asked, jerking his head to the left, indicating Randy.

I said evenly, 'As good as in church.'

He nodded solemnly.

'Two dollars for the needle; a dollar for the ink. Three dollars.'

I nodded agreement.

'I'll pay you this afternoon,' I said.

He did not seem to hear me but leaned in close, close enough that his breath was warm on my face and the cold, flaccid skin of his gut pressed against my arm.

'And I get first use of him when you two get divorced.'

I glanced at Randy before I nodded again, a barely perceptible movement of my head, the same nod I had first learned to use when trading currency for my clients.

* * *

They sat side by side on the lower bunk, Randy twisted around so that he could clasp the biker's fat knee with the hand he had marked.

'You dumb shit,' the biker said in a mild, almost friendly rebuke, 'you let the ink run.'

Randy did not reply but looked at me instead and smiled conspiratorially, as if we shared some private joke.

I shook my head and turned around, turning my back on both of them, leaning against the wrist-thick metal bars at the front of the cell. After a moment I noticed an unfamiliar man looking down at me from the guards' walkway above. Even standing still he seemed to be in motion, waving his arms, jerking his head, so I looked back at him curiously until he turned to say something to the person standing next to him, a woman, I was almost certain. Then she stepped up to look at me too, and I *was* certain. Her hair was dark brown, and it was fluffed fashionably, styled to appear unstyled. Her dark eyes were calm and level, holding my gaze so easily it was a moment before I noticed her gray suit, coat open enough to reveal the swell of her breasts, ripe in a way that reminded me I had served only one year of my three-year sentence.

Behind me, Randy said, alarmed, 'Hey, what are you doing?'

I turned quickly, in time to see him pull back his hand and slap the biker's arm ineffectively.

The biker laughed. A dark brown ball of tobacco rolled out of his mouth. He tried to catch it but missed; it fell onto his fat thigh and crumbled into a wet, fibrous wad.

Randy looked at me and said, 'He put my hand between his legs'—he hesitated, embarrassed, but incensed enough to get past it—'on his thing.'

Still chuckling, the biker unconcernedly picked up the wad of tobacco and put it back in his mouth.

'The boy won't keep his hand still.' His smile was suddenly mean and challenging. 'I was giving him something to hold on to.'

I took my hands out of my pockets and stared at him hard, putting a lot into it. He gave me his squinty-eyed look, chewed twice, looked away; angrily he grabbed Randy's hand and placed it firmly back on his knee.

I moved into the cell and stood in close to the bunks, my hands ready at my sides, waiting for the biker to look at me again. When he did I leaned in under the top bunk as if I were going to whisper to him, then grabbed his long, greasy hair. I yanked it back, slamming his head against the steel wall. He came up fast for a fat man, and as his weight shifted, I sprang back, yanking him forward and up, smashing his face against the welded metal frame of the upper bunk. Before he could fall back I yanked him forward again, throwing him sideways through the open cell door, where he hit the steel deck, coughing, choking on his tobacco, but rising quickly to his knees. I shot Randy a vicious look and stepped out of the cell, onto the strip.

The biker swung around as he got to his feet, crouched low, arms wide, an ugly red welt across his forehead. And he charged just like that, fast, trying to get his fat arms around me. I jabbed for the welt on his forehead, missed, caught his nose, kicked at his feet as he went past.

He turned quickly.

I heard Randy shout, 'Hey, you started it.'

The biker charged again.

I moved left, bumped Randy as he came out of the cell, pushed him out of the way.

One fat hand caught my shirt, and I hammered the arm hard, four quick shots to the elbow as he dragged me toward him and then threw me against the wall.

In close now, my feet off the ground dangling uselessly, ribs crushed, unable to breathe, I twisted his sodden bandanna with one hand, holding his head away, and I pounded that snarling, gap-toothed face. Around the edges of my vision I saw black. A guard's whistle sounded over and over in short, frantic, heart-pounding blasts.

* * *

I awoke on the floor, in time to see the dog burst into the cellblock, a big German shepherd straining against its leash so hard its front feet hardly touched the ground as it lunged, ears flat, lips curled back over those teeth, the snapping, frenzied sound of it reverberating off the steel floors and steel wall. Behind it came the guards in blue helmets, overhead lights flashing on their clear plastic visors as they screamed unnecessarily, 'Move it. Move it. Move it.' I rolled myself into a tight ball, face against the ringing steel.

I felt my ankles shackled, my arms pulled behind my back and cuffed. I was lifted to my feet, then, guided by a strong, firm hand, prodded by a hardwood stick, I was marched behind Randy and the biker to the lock-down cells, tiny, dark, one-man cells, where we were confined without any hope of privileges—exercise or showers—close enough together that I had to listen to the biker's obscene threats and Randy's adolescent whining. My whole body ached as I lay down on the narrow bunk; after a while I napped, the sound of angry voices intruding into a fitful sleep.

When I heard keys jingle and the hollow, metallic thump of the lock, in the first confused moments of waking I thought it was my wife coming in, out and back early on a Sunday morning: a run for pastries and the *Times-Picayune*. Just for a moment I could feel her next to me, legs and hips warm down my side, arms moving, turning pages noisily, skipping right through to the gossip columns before she began to read; slipping me a bite of her éclair, knowing I was waiting for it and would chew languorously, eyes closed, feeling as much as tasting the flaky, delicate crust and the smooth, rich whipped cream inside. Then I felt a tug on my foot and remembered: she would have to be back from the dead, too.

Without opening my eyes, I said angrily, 'What?'

A nasal voice came back sourly, loud and harsh: 'Man, what's your problem?'

I sat up enough to see at the foot of the bunk the same man I had seen watching me from the guards' walkway, in motion again, waving his long arms loose-jointedly as he said, 'Hey, chill out. This is Skinny.' He thumped a finger against his own chest, referring to himself as if to another person. His shrewd, almost feral eyes flickered around the cell, then stopped suddenly, locked on me. 'Show some respect. You are going to work for Skinny.'

'Is that right?' I said, starting to grin because I could picture him standing in my father's office, dressed as he was in dirty jeans and a sleeveless green fatigue jacket, unshaven, his hair matted with its own dark grease. I pictured him at work, boots tracking mud on the powder-blue carpet as he moved from desk to desk, reviewing exchange rates and approving transactions.

'That's right,' Skinny said, stating it as a fact. 'You are going to work undercover. That's different from being an informant. Get that straight. Informants tell on their friends. Undercovers don't have any friends.'

Skinny reached into his pocket, took out a can of beer, popped the top.

'Hey, Curbelo,' he said brightly, 'it'll get you out of jail.' He held the beer out to me, then shrugged indifferently. 'Or you can stay here until you're leaning back for the strip-searches—that's up to you.'

Curbelo, I thought. *How does he know that?*

I was christened Antonio Curbelo, but just

after my seventh birthday, after we had moved here from Honduras, my father changed our surname to Curbel—'just lopping off the extra vowel,' he had said—and shortly thereafter he had changed Antonio to Anthony, too, a change I had protested until I was the first Hispanic to attend one of New Orleans's more exclusive private schools. I confessed to one friend my real name, and after that I learned to fight.

'My name is Curbel,' I said, and took the beer, trying to appear casual about it. 'Tony Curbel.'

Skinny raised and dropped both shoulders at once in a way that caused his elbows to flap loosely at his sides.

'That's okay with Skinny,' Skinny said agreeably. 'He could give a shit. He's an equal opportunity employer.'

Ignoring him, I took a short swallow of the beer, eyes closed, savoring the nearly forgotten taste of it; then a long swallow, gulping it down greedily. When I opened my eyes I saw that Skinny was watching me. He smiled without humor, a hard glint in his eyes.

'It's easy to forget about the good things, right? Skinny knows. He did his time in here.'

'Yeah?' I said doubtfully, holding the can of beer, not offering it back.

'Yeah. Skinny did three years.' He put one

grimy canvas boot on the end of the bunk. 'In those days, cons didn't have civil rights. When they brought in the dogs they let the furry motherfuckers nibble at your pants.' He lifted the leg of his jeans to show a round, deep scar on the back and side of his calf. 'Those dogs are something, aren't they?' he added admiringly, looking at the scar himself before he pulled down the leg of his jeans. 'But Skinny got off easy—you'll get off even easier, thanks to Skinny.'

I took another swallow of the beer and ran my tongue over the inside of my lips.

'Why?' I asked, not really interested in any deal he could offer but letting him talk while I drank his beer.

He smiled knowingly.

'Because Skinny thinks you know what a shit your father is,' he said. 'Skinny thinks you know he's the one who put you in jail—'

'You know that for a fact?' I snapped.

Skinny eyed me coolly, looking me up and down.

'Skinny knows about your uncle, too,' he said. 'Skinny knows about the slaves he keeps out on Airline Highway.'

He shook his head slowly.

'You got one peach of a family, Curbel.'

I squeezed the beer can until the light aluminum flexed and popped.

Ni puedes imaginártelo, I thought. *You can't even imagine . . .*

CHAPTER TWO

My father and uncle grew up rich and pampered near Mochita, Honduras, the two youngest sons of a plantation-owning family, interested only in horses and hunting the twenty thousand acres their father owned. When he was nine, my father broke his first wild horse; that same year, my uncle, then ten years old, killed a panther with his bolt-action Enfield. They have both told me they grew up happy, exploring the land, getting to know the hundred or so families who worked it, rafting the river that ran through it, unencumbered by the responsibilities their father gave his two older sons, both of whom resented their leisure but who, after my grandfather died, inherited the land—shortly after which, my father and uncle, aged seventeen and eighteen respectively, were sent to the United States for school. And they were here, in their first year of exile at Tulane University, when their generation's war broke out.

It was the last of the simple wars, wars in which everyone was convinced we were *right*; and swept up in his classmates' patriotic fervor—and perhaps pursuing in another form the panther he had never had the chance to shoot—my father lied about both his nationality and his age and joined the marines. For his part, however, my uncle was swept away only by the loose—loose relative to Honduras, anyway—American women at Sophie Newcomb College and, observing that the competition for their affections was dwindling, literally, by the platoon, he stayed right where he was in New Orleans. So when my father returned from the war, wounded, decorated, and discharged with honor, he saw that while he had been advancing through the Pacific, shooting and being shot at by Japanese soldiers, his brother had been making *his* advances in a high-ceilinged Garden District apartment, a disparity of experience that, fueled by their essentially unlike personalities, began an antagonistic war between *them*. Their war has continued unabated for the forty-plus years since peace was declared in the Pacific, and as the sole witness to its brutality, I have learned to maintain an imperturbable neutrality.

I said to Skinny tiredly, 'They're not slaves.'

'Yeah? What do you call 'em?' He cocked his head to one side and regarded me with eyes that were alert and curious. When I did not reply, he said, 'Here's what Skinny thinks, Curbel: Skinny thinks your father is bringing in illegal aliens—particularly kids—and putting them to work. Skinny sees 'em all the time, bagging groceries, scraping peeling paint off houses, mowing rich people's lawns—'

'That's hardly slavery,' I interrupted.

'It is if he doesn't just employ them. And Skinny thinks he *owns* them.'

'My father—' I began.

'Your father,' he interrupted tersely, 'buys the kids in Central America, brings them here, gets them green cards, puts them to work. That's where your uncle comes in: he runs the employment agency that finds them jobs—the agency that takes a big percentage of their salary for as long as they work. And that's where *you* fit in, right? You took all that hard-earned cash and laundered it back through Central America.'

I looked away from him, at the peeling white paint on the wall.

'I didn't know where the money came from,' I said honestly. 'I thought it belonged to my clients.'

'Skinny can buy that,' Skinny said quickly. 'Who would suspect his own father?'

I felt his gaze on me but did not look up to return it.

'So the kids' parents are happy because they make a few dollars. The kids themselves are happy because they're in America wearing designer jeans and gold chains rather than barefoot and hungry at home—and even if they *aren't* happy they can't complain because they can always be sent back. All it takes is a word to Immigration and Naturalization and they're history, right? Back in banana-land, explaining to their parents why they have to return the money they got for them. The employers get cheap labor for their car washes and crayfish farms. The agency makes a bundle.'

He rolled his head back and rubbed the tip of his unshaven chin.

'What a scam,' he added, then dropped his hand. 'Shit, Skinny might like to have one himself. Have her keep the house clean. Do the laundry. Wax the car on Saturday.' He hitched up his jeans in a way that suggested he was just putting them back on. 'Any other personal services that came to mind.' He flashed a smile that made me think of a boy in a high school locker room.

'It's not that way,' I began sourly, shaking my head, resenting both his slurs and his lewd fabrications.

The smile remained on his face, but it became fixed and hard.

'Yeah? Then how is it, Curbel? You going to tell me your father's running a charity? Helping the poor kids find a better life?'

'It's not a charity,' I said patiently, 'and it's not slavery. It's a business—'

'The kids are a cash crop, Curbel, bought and sold like bananas or coffee—Skinny's surprised you didn't think to bring them in yourself.'

I felt a hot flush in my cheeks, the limit of my patience.

'Fuck you,' I said evenly.

A spark of anger appeared in Skinny's bright eyes, but it passed quickly. He smiled again, coldly, his lips sliding off his protruding front teeth.

'You think Skinny's jerking himself off?' he asked. 'Skinny *knows*, Curbel. He's got an informant.'

'As opposed to an undercover?' I asked sarcastically.

'Yeah, that's right, she *is* an informant. Because guess what? She's telling on her friends.'

I looked directly at him.

'My father?'

'Your father *and* your uncle,' he said, waving one loose-jointed arm in a gesture of disgust. 'They may be friends of hers, but partner, from where Skinny sits, they sure as shit aren't any friends of yours.' He turned toward the open cell door. 'Take a walk, Curbel. Skinny'll let you meet her.'

I saw exactly what he was doing, how he was setting the hook to reel me in; and for a moment I looked down and rolled the beer can back and forth between my palms, idly reading the label as it rotated past, thinking of my father and my uncle, of the history we shared.

Skinny said, 'Hey, Curbel: she may be an informant, but she's got a great body.'

* * *

As I followed him through the prison's noisy hallways, Skinny's arms flapped loosely at his sides; his long legs kicked out, overextended, as if he were stepping across deep furrows in an open field. But even as I smiled to myself about his comic, country-boy gait, that nagging thought of history stayed with me. I recalled how much I owed my father and my uncle, the debts I had incurred during the years I had spent shuttling back and forth between them. And more important, I knew the emotional sway they held over me and how they could use it mercilessly.

When I was four years old, in the same year the vaccine was discovered in America, a polio epidemic swept through Tegucigalpa, where we were living. My mother and my sister contracted it, and my father, with his brother's help, rushed all three of us to New Orleans. I was given the vaccine and was never affected. My sister recovered completely. Less than two weeks later, however, my mother died in an iron lung.

Although my father has told me he does not remember that I ever went to the hospital, my earliest memories—whether, in fact, they *are* memories or elaborate mental constructions—are of the hospital where my mother died. I can see very clearly the half-light in her room, her body encased in the cylindrical iron lung, the way she looked at me in the large viewing mirror fixed at an angle over her face. I can smell the odd combination of machine oil and disinfectant, rich and pungent; and I can hear the nightmarish sound of the mechanical lung working, pressing her body, the huge, almost human sound of its breathing a rhythmic, relentless thump-wheeze, thump-wheeze, thump-wheeze. Some part of all of us—of my father, my uncle, my sister, and me—is always there, in that room with my mother and that awful sound. It is the experience we share that isolates us and makes us close. And it is the weapon we turn on each other in anger, aiming it with the cold precision of a marksman aiming a bull-barreled rifle when he means to wound or to cripple, not to kill.

When I was a boy, the blind fury of my tantrums was uncontrollable, even by me. When I was seven I pounded a door to splinters simply because it was locked. At nine I beat up our maid when she called me a spoiled braggart, which undoubtedly I was. I began drinking when I was fourteen, driving when I was fifteen, and was first arrested at sixteen when I put my two new talents together and ran my father's Lincoln Continental sideways across two front yards before slamming it trunk-first into our neighbor's bedroom wall. While I recognized even then that my actions were reactions to the pain caused by my mother's death, I did not realize I was also trying to bond myself closer to those who shared her loss with me, demanding their attention, good or bad, regardless of the cost to their spirit or mine. After my father got me out of jail and beat me—for his humiliation as much as for my crime—as punishment he sent me to Mochita to work the fields.

'You behave like a peasant,' he reasoned, invoking the most disparaging word he knew, 'you'll live like a peasant.'

But the real punishment was not in going to Mochita: the real punishment was in having to come home.

Instead of making me work the fields, my grandmother allowed me to roam the mountains that surrounded the Curbelo plantation. For two months, carrying my uncle's old Enfield rifle on a sling over my shoulder, I explored the land, all the while pretending I was alone, self-sufficient, and fearless. I learned to love the lushness and abundance of that valley, the way fish flashed silver in its clear. fast-running river, how avocados big as melons grew wild, the way great hawks circled on currents in the spectacularly clear air. Most days my grandmother, dressed for riding in high boots, tan jodhpurs, and jacket, her shiny black hair coiffed perfectly, would find me in some remote spot, and she would act surprised, as if some random chance—and not the clear tracks of my sneakers left—had led her to me. She tethered her horse nearby, and, sitting on a brightly colored blanket, looking across the valley, we would eat the tortillas she brought, still warm, slathering them with fresh butter and sour cream, watching the clouds and the shadows they cast as they moved over the cane fields like great animals bounding.

With a great eye for details, and in a way that made me feel I knew them, my grandmother told me about the five generations of Curbelos who had lived on and worked that land. I got so I could recite the names of the men, their wives and children. I learned the small things about them—my great-uncle Lorenzo was missing a finger where a horse had kicked it off; my grandfather's cousin was the first woman in Honduras to wear her skirts above her ankles—and I learned about the events that had shaped their lives: revolutions, floods, poor crops, the American military invasion. My grandmother made me realize how different life was before electricity and gas-powered engines, and when I asked questions she gently corrected my Americanized Spanish before she answered in her quiet voice. On the day she told me about her two younger sons, placing my father and uncle into her chronology matter-of-factly, making them seem more a part of history than a part of the present, she also told me my father had called: I had to go home.

After my grandmother left me that day, I stayed on the mountainside and watched as the afternoon clouds clumped together and formed a thunderhead in the distance. To my teenager's fatalistic eye, that thunderhead seemed a portent of the most obvious sort, and I felt the valley was showing me both what there was in store for me when I returned to New Orleans and why my father and my uncle are as they are, very opposite in some ways, very much alike in others. Looking at that approaching storm. I tried to understand their differences, the way the whole environment of a house changes when one or the other enters, and to appreciate the precarious relationship between them. Then the first bolt of lightning flashed, a terrific gray-white light that split the sky, jaggedly, just at the front edge of the clouds, and I saw in it the fearsome, devastating capacity for violence that is so much a part of them both.

'*Yo soy Curbelo*,' my grandmother had replied when I asked how she had survived the traumatic events of her long life. 'I am a Curbel.'

'*Yo soy Curbelo*,' I repeated thereafter, whenever I was doubtful of myself.

When I said it this time, actually mumbling it out loud, Skinny was there to cast a suspicious glance at me.

He said, 'She's in here'; then he turned into the small office the doctor used when he visited the prison on Tuesdays and Thursdays.

In the middle of the room was a worn examination table covered in black vinyl. On the floor was a worn gray carpet. Overhead, two bare fluorescent tubes hummed quietly.

Skinny's informant was the woman I had seen standing next to him on the guards' walkway; up close she held my gaze as easily as she had at a distance, her dark eyes confident and level, one eyebrow arched slightly higher than the other, curious. She wore a conservative gray suit, coat open, and a sheer white blouse without buttons. Her nose was short and straight. She sat on a stool placed near one end of the examination table, legs crossed, purse open beside her.

Skinny said, 'This is Stacey Veldran,' pronouncing her name with the vowels hard, Anglicized. 'She knows who you are.'

He made a careless gesture with his hand. 'She works for your uncle.'

He stepped to the end of the examination table opposite her and took hold of one of the stainless steel stirrups affixed there.

'What the shit they got these in here for?' he asked idly.

An annoyed look crossed Stacey Veldran's face, a slight twist to her lips.

She asked me, 'Why are you in jail?'

Skinny said quickly, 'One of his clients packed a thousand pounds of marijuana in with his shipment of Honduran mahogany, right, Curbel?' He shifted his glance from the stirrup to me, then on to Stacey Veldran. 'Tony couldn't get anybody to believe he didn't know about it since he had inspected the shipment and paid the freight. Nobody could believe he could be so dumb. But Skinny believes him. Skinny knows how dumb people can be.'

He smiled brightly.

'There's a bit more to it,' I said.

Stacey Veldran's eyebrows arched slightly, inquiringly or skeptically, it was hard to tell which.

'Who put the marijuana into the shipment?' she asked.

'He says he doesn't know,' Skinny replied for me. 'But Skinny knows. So do you.'

She gave him a withering look.

Skinny shrugged and looked back at me. 'She wants to run it down to you herself, Curbel. Tell you all about your family. Let you hear about your *roots*. That's why she's looking at Skinny like that: he's spoiling her surprise.'

Skinny smiled rudely at Stacey, spun the stirrup, took two long steps toward the door.

'Skinny said okay to that. He'll be back in half an hour.'

At the door he paused, one hand on the doorknob, one hand waving at his side.

'Keep your knees together, Veldran,' he said. 'The guy's been in jail a year, you know?'

Stacey Veldran pursed her lips slightly, and little lines of irritation appeared on her forehead.

Skinny stepped through the door so she could not see him, winked at me lewdly, closed the door.

When I lookd back at her, Stacey Veldran sat up straight and tiredly moved her purse to her lap.

I watched the sheer fabric pull taut over the swell of her breasts.

With one hand she held her purse open on her lap, and with the other she dug around in it, annoyed, it seemed, that she was not able to find what she was looking for. A short, deep furrow appeared between her eyebrows. After a moment she took out a pack of cigarettes, removed one from the pack, put the pack on the table. A lighter surfaced soon thereafter, and when her cigarette was lit, she inhaled deeply, then blew a long, slanting plume of smoke at the ceiling and allowed her eyes to follow it, looking up at the welded steel plates that made up the ceiling. She kept her lighter in her hand and flipped and turned it.

She said, 'I don't know who's responsible for your being here.' She turned her head to look at me. 'Here in jail.'

I raised and dropped one shoulder in a dismissive shrug.

'You work for my uncle?' I asked, making it a question by the way I said it, doubtfully.

'Yes,' she replied coolly. 'I work for your uncle. I have for almost twenty years.'

Her eyes flicked about, looking for something.

I saw a plastic ashtray on the doctor's small desk, stepped over and picked it up, placed it on the table near her pack of cigarettes. Up close to her I noticed two things: that beneath the make-up and the expensively tailored clothes she was a bit older than I had first supposed and that there was downlike hair along her neck, beneath her ear, the kind of hair you can hardly feel with your lips.

She said, 'Thank you,' and waited for me to move away.

But I stayed near, near enough to savor the rich sweetness of her perfume.

One hand went to the collar of her blouse and pulled it close, a modest gesture that somehow drew attention to the bare skin beneath the sheer fabric.

She said, 'I was among the first illegals your father brought into this country. I started to work for your uncle when I was ten years old.'

It was my turn to raise my eyebrows, and I did, trying to convey the same inquiring skepticism she had turned on me before.

'Before that my father worked for your uncles, the two in Honduras. My father was a cane-cutter on their plantation. We lived in Mochita.'

'I've been there,' I said, 'not to Mochita itself but to the plantation.'

'No, you wouldn't go to Mochita,' she said softly, almost to herself, then her voice got stronger and she added, 'Why should you? You're a Curbelo.'

It was in and out of her eyes when she glanced at me, resentment, uncertainty, and something else that was deeper—fear, perhaps, or hatred.

'There's nothing there for you,' she continued. 'Mochita is one of those little towns with only a church, a supply store, and a cantina. There's no electricity, no running water, no anything except a view of your uncles' land in the valley. You can see it from every window, their land and their big white house.'

She flicked an ash into the ashtray, took a final pull on her cigarette, mashed it out.

'My mother is still there.'

My eyes were on hers. There was something in her tone that her words did not explain.

'And your father?' I asked. 'Is he still cutting cane?'

She fixed me in a hard, challenging stare. 'My father is dead. He was killed in a tractor accident when I was nine.'

I looked away from her bitter stare to the worn steel plates on the floor.

'If he hadn't been killed I'd still be there, too. He would never have allowed me to leave.'

For a moment neither of us said anything, then she went on, her voice quieter now but just as hard, 'Do you know what I remember most about my father? I remember his dirty feet, how gray dust coated them and how it cracked near his toes, like skin.'

The more I listened to her, the more I became certain she was up to something, playing me toward some end. I looked up enough to see her examine her own foot, pulling the shiny black toe of her shoe back toward herself so that the tall high heel slipped free of her heel, leaving the shoe dangling.

'The year after my father died, your father brought me here, and I went to work for your uncle.'

'What do you do for him?' I asked, looking again at her face, watching her.

'I do anything he wants me to do,' she said evenly, unambiguously, careful to look me right in the eye. 'Anything at all. Your uncle is very good to me.'

It was a tone she had practiced, a tone intended to shock and to insinuate; and I very nearly laughed out loud at it because the sequence was so familiar to me, the manipulative one-two of tacit guilt and implied association—I am, after all, my father's son. I did not believe her for a second.

'Really? Anything at all?' I said, mocking her, smiling coldly, and pointedly allowing my eyes to wander over her. 'And my uncle wants you here? Informing on him?'

She dropped my cold glance and started to reach for her pack of cigarettes, but I caught her wrist and held it, forcing her to look at me.

'He's in trouble,' she said angrily. 'This is the only way I know to help him.'

'What sort of trouble?' I pressed.

She held my gaze for a moment, then stared hard at my hand on her wrist, her meaning very clear.

I released her by throwing my arm out in exaggerated contempt, throwing her hand with it, harder than I had intended, hard enough that she started to fall, and I grabbed her coat to steady her.

A quick recoiling fear came into her, a cowering, as if she expected physical harm: her face became drawn and pale, her eyes wide with silent, helpless terror.

Puzzled, I stepped away from her and turned away and back, putting my hands in my pockets as I did so.

She did not look at me.

I studied her face, watching the color come back into it, the terror recede.

'Are you okay?' I asked.

She did not reply but shook her head sharply, as if to clear it; then she looked at me, and I saw her expression was again composed, her dark eyes hard and level, only her paleness revealing the strength of the fear she had felt.

She adjusted the bracelet on her wrist, and asked, 'Why did you attack that man? The man in your cell?'

I did not understand the sudden shifts in her, and I was wary of them.

'The fat guy?' I asked.

She nodded.

'I wasn't attacking him. I was defending myself.'

She sat quietly, watching me.

'It's difficult to explain,' I added, off balance, stumbling. 'There are rules in here, rules to doing *good time*.'

She did it again, arched her eyebrow in her maddeningly skeptical way.

'That kid you saw in my cell, he's new. His name is Randy. I shouldn't have taken him in, but I did; and now he's my responsibility. The fat guy wants him, and if I let him take him, he'll assume I'm next. That's the way it works in here. Give away your dessert, you're giving away your jacket, too.' I shrugged. 'Show any weakness, ever, and you may as well bend over.'

She accepted that readily, without question, her features softening thoughtfully.

She said, 'That's not too hard to understand.'

'Besides that, he's ugly,' I said seriously, 'and he chews tobacco with his mouth open.'

I waited for a smile that never came.

Stacey Veldran looked at her cigarettes, decided against one, put her hands in her lap.

'Have you ever heard of a man named Esperoza? A banker?'

I shook my head, no, and asked, 'With which bank?'

'He's the chief account executive for the Banco de Santander, Panama City.'

I shook my head again.

'But you went there often, didn't you?'

'To Panama,' I said, 'not to the Banco de Santander—there are over a hundred banks in Panama City.'

'I see,' she said softly. 'I didn't realize . . .' There was genuine surprise in the way she said it, her words trailing off, surprise and relief. 'It's not important.'

She picked up her cigarettes and her lighter and put both in her purse.

'I may have made a mistake,' she said, and

without another word to me, she stood up and left, pausing at the door only long enough to arrange herself, fluffing her hair, straightening her coat.

Perplexed, I watched her go, wondering whether her exit was a curt dismissal or a calculated ploy—wondering what it meant to me. I leaned back against the examination table; then, after a few minutes, I moved the ashtray and stretched out on top of the table, my feet dangling over the end, hands interlaced on my chest.

In my mind the town of Mochita was built around a single steep road. There was one large church, one small store, a cantina with a broad front porch, and a fiesta-terrace strung with faded decorations. Their bells clanking, goats wandered about freely between the tin-roofed houses; children ran about barefoot. And though I tried in different ways to put Stacey Veldran into that town—as a skinny young girl in a tattered dress, all elbows and knees, dark eyes huge in a small face; as a teenager visiting home, prematurely worldly-wise and world-weary, in designer jeans and a white cotton top—I could not make her fit, not well: she was at the same time both too self-possessed and too easily frightened, too much the product of a city. So I put her back at the door, fluffing her hair, leaving; then back on the stool, legs crossed, the curve of her calf sheathed in her shiny, silvery stockings. I thought of the white disk of her kneecap, of the warmth that would be between her thighs, the qualities of it, slick nylon-warmth first, rough to the touch, then above the stockings smooth and soft, deeper warmth, pliable, moist.

From the doorway, Skinny said in his rude nasal voice, 'What are you doing on the table, Curbel? Greased up for your Pap smear? Want Skinny to take a look at your tubes?'

I rolled my head enough to see him, his long arms in motion again, an amused smile playing across his shrewd face.

'See, Skinny told you she had a great body.'

He put his hands on his hips.

'So, Curbel, you ready to get out of here?'

CHAPTER THREE

The clothes I had worn into prison over a year before were waiting for me in the property room, neatly wrapped in brown paper, sealed with brown paper tape. The old trusty who retrieved the package for me set it down gently, respectfully, on the worn wooden counter, blew the dust off it, and carefully unwrapped it; then he set my socks, underwear, shoes, and tie to one side and put my slacks, shirt, and jacket on hangers, smoothing the wrinkles with his hand.

'I bet you'll be glad to get into these,' he said in a friendly way, referring to my street clothes. He ran his fingers under the lapel of my jacket and added, 'You never forget the first time you get out. Never.'

I smiled faintly.

He went to a file cabinet, took out a yellow form, glanced at it as he went into the wire mesh cage behind the counter. After a moment he returned with a large Manila envelope and handed it to me.

'You have to sign for your things,' he said, and slid the yellow form across the counter.

I signed where he indicated, tore open the envelope, dumped it on the counter. My wallet, watch, and keys fell out, and for a long moment I looked at them curiously, realizing what they represented, seeing them very clearly, as if they belonged to someone else.

'Is something missing?' the trusty asked.

'No,' I said, and picked up my watch, admiring the fact that it was still running, the second hand jerking from one second to the next.

I placed the watch on my wrist and felt the small buckle slip into its worn, familiar place.

'There's a mirror behind you,' the trusty said.

I changed clothes before I turned to look at myself, studying my image in the full-length mirror as I knotted my tie and tightened the knot into my conservative button-down collar.

I noted with some satisfaction that I looked trim in my tan slacks, white shirt, and blue blazer. My dark wiry hair now was shot through with gray. My jaw was angular and strong. My skin was pale, almost gray, too long without sunshine. A year before what I liked best about my face was that I could look at my eyes and see fun in them, a ready good humor; I liked the creases that showed I smiled often. Now my eyes were flat, dull brown, and humorless. But I knew the good humor was in there somewhere. I could feel it behind that hard face looking back at me. I could almost see it when I tried to wink at myself but could not bring it off: what I got looked more like a twitch, a tense spasm, and deep down I caught a gleam, a spark of self-mocking amusement.

'Is that it, buddy?' I asked myself. 'That's all you have?'

I put my wallet and keys into my pockets.

⋆ ⋆ ⋆

There was a dreamlike quality to the small events that followed, a sense of heightened perception as my leather heels rang on the steel floors, a guard completed a lengthy form, the doors and gates buzzed open. Then

Skinny was beside me, talking, and we were outside in the sunshine on the corner of Tulane and South Broad, the sky high and blue overhead, cars passing close by at high speed. I felt the sunshine more than anything else, the way it warmed my dark jacket and put white behind my eyelids. I felt the light on my skin.

Skinny left me for a few minutes, explaining that he had to see someone in an office nearby before he got his car, so I waited for him there on the sidewalk, idly walking to the corner and back, looking around, glancing at the Criminal Courts Building and the parish prison just behind it. Around the prison there was a very high chain-link fence topped with coils of razor wire, and I recalled the first time I had seen that vicious fence and the heavy, squat stone building inside it: my father and I had been in his car, parked on the curb just outside the gate on the day I had reported to jail.

My father had said, 'I will miss you,' as he looked straight ahead, through the windshield, carefully avoiding the view of the prison through the window on my side. His thinning gray hair was uncharacteristically out of place, ruffled, a few strands falling down across his forehead.

'You know where you can find me,' I had replied very drily.

Behind his brown-rimmed glasses his eyes

were both sad and resolute.

'I will not visit you in jail,' he said softly.

'Even though I'm going to jail for you?' I asked.

He did not reply to that but turned on the car and allowed it to run at idle, looking at his watch as he did so, making a point of it.

'It is time for you to go in,' he said.

I felt anger well up in me, anger and deep hurt.

He started to say something more, but I got out of the car before he could, throwing the door open, stepping out quickly, slamming the door shut.

The electric window slid down smoothly. He had held my gaze as long as he had been able, then he had put his car in gear and had driven away, leaving me there on the curb, looking after him long after he had gone out of sight.

Then as now I could not believe it: no father would send his own son to jail, not for money.

Across that same broad avenue I saw Skinny get into an old battered Ford and make an illegal U-turn, coming back to get me. When I got into the car with him, the vinyl upholstery was hot to the touch. The air-conditioning blew hot, getting cooler. The ride across town passed in one long moment, a collage of images and bright colors I could not seem to integrate.

Skinny explained that he was dropping me at my uncle's shop so that I could ask about the agency and find out how it worked, how the illegal aliens were brought in and farmed out for a profit. He wanted the names of the businesses involved and the dollar amounts and dates of the charges. And I was supposed to find out about the banker Stacey Veldran had mentioned, the account executive named Esperoza, why he was important. But I only half-listened as Skinny went on because I had no intention of informing on my family. I had my own agenda, and even as I considered it, I felt the seething anger course through me; I would find out who had put me in jail and why—and then I would consider what to tell Skinny.

As he pulled to the curb and stopped I began my evasion, explaining to him about my uncle, how he had never been known to give a straight answer. But he did not want to hear it.

'You find out or you're back in the joint,' he said, and snapped his fingers. 'Just like that.'

His eyes were bright green in the sunlight, flecked with yellow.

'Is that all?' I asked, putting weariness into my voice.

He reached across me and pushed my door open.

I got out and turned back to face him, bent

from the waist, looking in through the open door.

Skinny rolled down his window, spit out his chewing gum, rolled the window back up.

'Skinny wonders about you, Curbel,' he said.

I did not reply to him but looked at him tiredly, impatiently, careful not to remark that I wondered about him, too, about his rather curious association with the police, the status he could not—or would not—explain.

'Skinny wonders why you haven't asked about your live-in. The girl did.' He draped one long arm across the back of the seat. 'She said, "What will happen to the boy? To Randy?" But from you Skinny hasn't heard a peep.'

I held his hot gaze only a moment, then stood up straight and shut the car door.

CHAPTER FOUR

My uncle's shop was in an old, faded, stucco-covered cottage not much larger than a two-car garage. The cottage had settled noticeably, bowing along its chain-wall base so that the roof sagged and the walls drooped in a way that made it seem it was folding in on itself, slowly subsiding behind the dark green fence that separated it from the street.

Around the two front windows woody vines grew up cracks in the wall. A worn block of granite served as a step up to the French door entrance.

I knocked and waited, knocked again, but there was no answer. I tried the door, which was open.

Inside, a wall divided the cottage in half, front and back. In front, the floor was covered with a pallid yellow linoleum that had curled up in the corners and near the bases of the adjustable barber's chairs. Affixed to the dividing wall were large mirrors. Awaiting my uncle's arrival I sat in one of the barber's chairs, ankles crossed, hands on the tubular armrests, feeling the scabrous spots where rust had broken through the thin covering of chrome. Looking around casually, I noticed that the stucco on the walls was crumbling in places, exposing in blisterlike patches the soft orange brick beneath, and that, I assumed, accounted for the musty smell of undisturbed dust that commingled with the pungent-sweet fragrances of the shampoos, gels, and sprays my uncle used when he cut and styled hair. Waiting there, my memory triggered by the shop's distinctive odor, I recalled the first time I had come to the shop, the day I had returned from Mochita. The auspicious beginning.

* * *

I was sixteen years old, tanned dark brown by the Honduran sun, strong, healthy, and not quite ready to go back to my father's house; so I had called my uncle from the airport and asked if I could come by to see him before I went home. His answer, though largely unintelligible grunts, had seemed positive, so I found his address in the phone book, took a cab, and was in his shop less than an hour later. I remembered that I had waited patiently in the empty shop—just as I was waiting now—expecting then, however, that at any moment the door to the back of the shop would open and my uncle would emerge, glad to see me, muttering apologies for the delay. But after waiting fifteen minutes I had pushed open the door myself and peered in, seeing even before my eyes fully adjusted to the dim light that the room was in astonishing disarray. Cushions were scattered helter-skelter, singly and in pairs. Electric cords snaked across the floor. In one corner the chairs had been pushed together and stacked haphazardly in a pile that included a small table, a trash can, and a floor lamp. Two tripods topped by expensive cameras tilted at precarious angles. I had seen my uncle in striped boxer shorts, sprawled across the fold-out bed, looking around at the sound of the door squeaking open, his face swollen with sleep, eyes bloodshot, beard mashed flat on one side, asking irritably even before he saw who it was, 'What do you want?'

'You said I could come by,' I had replied uncertainly, taken aback.

'You're early,' he said gruffly.

'Actually,' I replied defensively, 'you're late—I said I would be here by noon.'

Slowly he pushed himself up until he was on all fours.

'That,' he said, his head drooped between his arms, apparently examining a spot on the bed, 'is a matter of time. What I'm referring to'—he kicked one leg off the bed, somehow toppling to a reasonably upright sitting position—'is a matter of tim*ing*.'

I considered that, realizing it was, at that moment, a hard point to argue—and wondering if I shouldn't simply head out to my father's house. I was embarrassed for my uncle, embarrassed by both his condition and the condition of the room. I knew then why I had never been invited to visit, why he always came to my father's house.

As he had fallen to his sitting position my uncle's penis had slipped out of the slit in his shorts, and he looked at it curiously, humorously, as if he had just discovered it, and said, 'For such a harmless-looking son of a bitch, you sure cause a lot of trouble.'

He tucked his penis back into his shorts and peered up through his eyebrows, scrutinizing the damage to the room, then seeming to see me for the first time.

'You wouldn't believe the night I had,' he said. His voice was a mix of disbelief and pride, addressed to me in a way that made me feel I was a co-conspirator.

'Uncle,' I replied candidly, 'I'd believe anything. Look at this place.'

He smiled, then thoughtfully scratched his beard with his fingertips.

'I think,' he said, 'you are old enough to quit calling me uncle.'

'What should I call you?' I asked.

'Call me by my name,' he replied, yawning and stretching elaborately, extending his arms straight out, then bending them as he arched and rotated his back. 'Call me Ellis.'

'Okay,' I agreed.

My uncle saw that I was again looking around, surveying the striking disorder, and said, 'I was taking pictures of two beautiful young girls,' as if that explained it all.

'So?' I asked casually, trying to sound older than I was, knowing there had to be more to the story—and wanting to hear it.

'So I moved the furniture,' he said, smiling again.

When my uncle stood up it was with difficulty. He pushed down hard with his left leg and threw his torso forward so that his right leg remained straight. I saw a jagged white scar that ran from his hip to his ankle, a deep depressed scar that indicated what must have been a serious injury.

He saw that I was watching, and said, 'That's a war wound, of a sort.'

I said nothing because I knew very well—my father had told me often enough—that he had never been to war.

Once standing, he limped about, throwing the scattered cushions onto the bed, unplugging the heavy-gauge electric cords, returning the floor lamp to the floor.

I felt out of place watching him move about awkwardly, so I put my hands in my pockets and pretended to look out the window, catching glimpses of him out of the corners of my eyes.

Barefoot, my uncle was six-six to the top of his tightly curled hair. His hair, like his beard, had been mashed flat by the pillow, and from the front his head was a flattened circle off-center to his face. His lips moved loosely over his teeth, and I realized he was likely adjusting a bridge. With surprising delicacy he straightened the tripods and started to rewind the film in the cameras.

'About twenty years ago,' he began, his attention on the camera but talking about the scar on his leg, 'before you were even a gleam in your father's eye, I found out that a friend of mine was having a party on his boat. That whore dog. I'd been to *his* parties, but for this one he had invited *my* sweetheart, a beautiful young girl—beautiful but naïve. So I decided to crash the party, sort of to drop in unannounced. The problem was, by the time I got to the dock the son of a snake had already taken the boat and was somewhere on the lake.'

He finished with the first camera, extracted the canister of film, moved on to the second.

'So I hurried out to the airport to find a pilot who would give me a short course in parachutes, then fly me around until I spotted the boat. That's simple enough, you'd think, but the real problem was that by the time I found a pilot and convinced him of the merit of my plan, he was as drunk as I was; and when finally I got up the nerve to jump out of the airplane I wasn't even over water; I didn't just miss the boat, I missed the whole goddamn lake.'

Knowing he had my interest, he paused. He removed the film from the second camera, fussed with the lens, shook his head as if dissatisfied with some setting.

'I hit a parked car first—that wasn't so bad except that I broke the windshield, which I had to pay for—but then I couldn't unharness the damn parachute. The wind caught it, and it dragged me half the length of Lakeshore Drive before it snagged on a vegetable truck, an old toothless guy driving it who thought maybe he'd hit a patch of fog, because he drove back the other way, the way I'd just come, pulling me along like a loose tailpipe.'

My uncle shook his head sideways, then gave a backward glance, smiling slyly.

'It worked like a charm. I couldn't have planned it any better.'

He put the two film canisters on the pilaster-style mantel, then turned around and hitched up his boxer shorts as he took a stiff-legged step forward, serious now, expounding.

'See, here was a guy who had spent a hundred, maybe two hundred thousand dollars on a fancy boat with all the trimmings—teak deck, brass rails, big color television set in the stateroom—and there was the girl he had bought the boat to impress up in my hospital room feeling guilty as all hell that she had ever even seen that boat, much less gone out on it, giving me rubdowns for the price of replacing a windshield in a three-year-old Dodge.' Feigning a grimace that dissolved to an artful, contented grin, he rolled his head back and closed his eyes. 'Oh, not quite there, sweetheart. Up a bit higher, to the left, that's it. A little slower now.'

When my uncle again opened his eyes he smiled easily and winked, a candid wink that I liked because it suggested not only that some license had been taken with the story but also that he was aware of his licentiousness, preferring to tell a colorful story to an accurate one but, in the telling, not confusing the fact and the fancy of it.

'And that,' he had said with finality, 'is what happened to my leg—there are all sorts of wars, Tony.'

I held my index finger to my lower lip, a perplexed look on my face.

'I didn't ask about your leg,' I said.

'You didn't have to: I could tell by your expression that you were curious.'

'Oh,' I said.

'Wait out front,' my uncle suggested. 'I'll be with you in a minute.'

I saw what he was doing, how he was steering me away from any further questions about his activities of the night before, and I wanted to let him know I knew it.

'Does this mean,' I asked, feeling very clever, 'you're not going to tell me about the two beautiful young girls?'

My uncle had not been amused by my cleverness. He thought my remark over for a moment, stepped near, and glared down at me.

'That,' he said, 'is exactly what that means.'

I had felt myself flush under the intensity of his gaze, and I had turned, gone back into the shop, and after first removing a black leather portfolio from the red vinyl seat, had sat in the same barber's chair I was sitting in now. The portfolio was as thick as a big city telephone directory, and I allowed it to rest heavily on my lap without opening it, idly rubbing the pebble-grain leather as I tried to understand what had prompted my impertinence.

When my uncle appeared he had dressed in pale blue pants and a short-sleeved, loose-fitting white shirt with low pockets in front and a squared-off hem. It was the sort of shirt made to be worn untucked, casual, but embellished with epaulets and elaborate stitching. An oversize Saint Christopher's medal hung around his neck and dangled into a puff of chest hair. Water stood in drops like ornaments in his bushy hair.

'Did you really call?' he asked, taking a plastic cloth from a peg on the wall and snapping it menacingly.

'I called from the airport,' I affirmed.

He wrapped the cloth around my neck and almost choked me with it, clinching it tightly and fastening it.

I worked two fingers under the collar and popped it loose.

'Okay,' he said, and shrugged nonchalantly. 'The hair goes down your neck.'

'I don't really need a haircut,' I protested halfheartedly.

He did not bother to reply but reached over to the shelf under the mirror and picked up long, pointed scissors and a fine-toothed comb, which he dropped into the waist-level pocket of his shirt. With the fingers of both hands he pinched my hair in various places and pulled it out, away from the scalp, examining it.

'How is your grandmother?' he asked dutifully.

'She's well,' I said.

'And your sister?'

'I haven't seen her. I've been in Mochita.'

'Working the fields?' He looked over my head into the mirror.

'Not exactly,' I admitted.

'You better not tell your father,' he advised gruffly. He turned to his right and rummaged along the crowded shelf under the mirror, picking through the array of bottles, jars, and tubes that were there. He picked up one, a plastic spray bottle, then turned back, tilted the chair to his liking, and began to spray my hair with cold liquid. 'When your grandfather sent us to the fields, the old goat really made us work.'

I did not know what to say to that, so I sat quietly, listening to the sometimes slow, sometimes rapid, snip of the scissors, watching in the mirror as he hobbled sullenly from one side of the chair to the other. At that moment I regretted the impulse that had caused me to call. My uncle did not seem particularly pleased to see me, and I felt I was being merely tolerated, an unwelcome guest who could not be refused. I cast about for something to say but could think of nothing but family—and family did not seem to help. It was not until he again adjusted the chair, shifting me enough that the heavy portfolio slipped in my lap, that I thought to ask about it.

'What's in here?' I said, lifting the portfolio from beneath the plastic sheet, holding it in one hand.

My uncle was hunched over as he worked his left hand across my head and with the scissors in his right snipped the spines of hair that appeared between his fingers.

I saw him start, recover, finish a cut.

'Go ahead, take a look,' he said, then added tersely, 'but keep the hair off the pictures.'

I felt I was intruding even more, but now it was either open the portfolio or risk compounding his ill humor; so I held the portfolio at arm's length and opened it, curious to see that the first eight-by-ten black-and-white photograph was of a mausoleum, a simple massive granite vault with the bronze figure of a seated female figure to one side of the doorway.

Behind me my uncle said, 'That's the tomb of our late mayor, Dutton N. Landrial, otherwise known as "Standstill" Landrial. Look at the sculpture of the woman. She's supposed to be weeping, I think—whether for him or for what he did to the city I never could decide.'

I did not reply but studied the photograph, admiring the extraordinary clarity of it, a clarity that gave a feel to the materials, the smoothness of the polished granite surface, the heaviness of the bronze. A shadow so black it was luminous hid the door of the tomb, and it took me a moment to realize that the shadow was the focus of the picture, capturing the eerie sense of what it was like behind the sealed door, the sense of absolute darkness, cold, and silence.

For a moment I thought of my mother in that same absolute darkness and felt her loss, a painful twinge of it.

I felt my uncle looking at me, but when I lifted my head he shifted his gaze back to the photograph.

'That's what I think of, too,' he said, reading my thought. 'Your mother. She was such a beautiful woman, so full of life.'

I did not want to hear it.

'She's dead,' I said angrily, 'rotting in her grave.'

He slapped me once, hard, on the back of my head.

I felt a fury rise in me. I started to push myself out of the chair, but he put one big hand on my shoulder and held me down, glaring at me, towering over me. He did not say anything, but his own anger was there in his eyes.

'Turn the page,' he ordered.

I jerked my head away.

'Turn the page,' he said again, more gently.

I felt the anger drain as quickly as it had come, replaced by a sadness so deep it seemed to touch the core of me. I felt a burning in my eyes.

I turned the page.

The photograph that followed was so completely different from the first that it required an adjustment of sorts simply to perceive it, to form the image to a comprehensible picture, and I found myself really looking, trying to see.

The print was in color, slightly blurred by the movement of the subject, an attractive young woman, her hair wet and combed forward covering one eye, a telephone receiver held to her ear. It was her movement to the telephone that had caused the blur, but the focus on her face was sharp and showed a radiant smile that included the visible eye, the smile an expression of happiness so undiluted it seemed to offset the picture that preceded it.

'She had just had a big fight with her boyfriend,' my uncle explained, 'and came in for a cut, a new look, she said, to help her get over the rotten bastard. I'd just washed her hair when the phone rang, and she bolted for it. I grabbed the camera and got her right then, bounced the flash off the ceiling—that's why the light on her face is so diffuse.' He shook his head with feigned exasperation. 'I blurred the shot hurrying, and she was on the phone so long her hair dried. I had to put her back in the sink.'

He reached down and turned the page himself to side-by-side pictures of an old plantation house. The photographs showed the front elevation of the house before and after a devastating fire.

'It was called the Maison Rouge,' he said. 'It was built in 1825 by a cotton planter who gave it as a wedding present to his daughter. Nice present. It had twenty-three rooms, every one of them huge. The walls were all two feet thick.'

Again I admired the extraordinary, almost dreamlike clarity of the photographs, studying first the picture taken before the fire.

'During the Civil War,' my uncle continued, 'Union troops used the house as a yellow fever hospital, so no one went near it for years because they were afraid it was infected. After that vagrants lived in it. Lightning hit it about ten years ago, and it burned.' He pointed with his comb to the right-hand page. 'That's what's left.'

Even now I can recall that there was an evocative quality to the photographs, the suggestion of an age lost in time; and although I was only sixteen years old and very likely unable to realize my own response, particularly in the photograph taken after the fire, there was a captivating requirement for the observer to participate, to engage the imagination to recreate the destroyed parts of the house, picturing it as it was, new, then inevitably comparing the construction image to the left-hand picture, the picture of the house whole, a hundred years neglected. One moment it seemed I was looking forward from the past; the next, backward from the present, my perceptions shifting. And although I did realize I was still affected by the residue of the strong emotion I had felt a few minutes before, still I could not shake the idea that in combination the photographs entangled time, making past, present, and future seem equally coexistent, equally *current*, so that even the previous photographs, the tomb and the woman's happiness, life and death, seemed somehow interchangeable, phases in a continuum.

My uncle leaned forward, closed the portfolio, took it and put it on a shelf.

'Anger,' he said, 'is not the only way to deal with loss.'

His eyes were at the same time both understanding and hard, seeming to see right into me, sharing my hurt; and in the acknowledgment of that shared pain a bond formed between us, a tacit understanding. I remembered how, after a moment, he could not hold my gaze, how his face began to crumple and how to hide it he hobbled clumsily to the cabinet over the shampoo sink and took out tequila and triple sec, mixing margaritas—his tonics—in large plastic cups intended for compounding curling fluid, handing me one before he drank himself, deeply. And I remembered how in the years that followed my haircuts became something near to ritual for us both: my uncle opening with an outrageous story; a quick trim; a new photograph displayed or an old one reviewed; an afternoon of tonics and easy talk, the topics as varied and as random as the subjects of the photographs. Sitting now in the barber's chair I could revive the conversations in detail, imagining even my uncle's facial expressions and the nuances of his speech.

Those afternoons in my uncle's shop were a good time for me, a time when I relaxed, listening to his seemingly endless stock of stories, learning: how he had dropped out of Tulane and joined the navy to see the world but had been trained as a barber and assigned to the Belle Chase Naval Air Station, less than thirty miles from New Orleans; how he had finally married the girl he had parachuted to see on the boat but that the marriage had failed when he had started to cut women's hair, too; how he had begun to take pictures simply to record his haircuts but had discovered women behaved quite differently in front of a camera . . .

Hearing those stories in that shop that had remained mostly unchanged in the intervening years I gained a new sense of my father and him, understanding them at about the same age I was then, when they were sent to New Orleans to struggle with the new language and new customs; when they returned home to Honduras to discover that they had become strangers there, too; when they learned the devastating effects of polio. And I remembered that it was after one of his stories that I had asked my uncle—had come right out with it when I felt particularly relaxed, as if removed to another age—why my mother's death had affected him so deeply since he was, after all, only an in-law. And right away I had known I had made a very bad mistake: I had seen it in the way my uncle's eyes had clouded, just momentarily, but enough; I had felt it in the way my blood ran cold with the realization that he had to have been more to her than a brother-in-law—enough more, in fact, that his brother would hate him for it and would carry a bitter grudge for nearly forty years. And when I wondered if he had pictures of her, too, I knew with cool certainty that, whatever had happened between them, I did not want to know it. I had heard enough stories.

After that, I allowed my visits with my

uncle to taper off and finally stopped them completely, seeing him only at my father's house when he came to visit on holidays or to go to church. I resented him for changing my image of my mother, tingeing it with sordidness; and I did not doubt that he resented me, too, both for forcing him to replay that regretful time—and to review its consequences—and for giving him companionship, then taking it away.

* * *

The windows in the French doors rattled when my uncle entered awkwardly, stepping up with his good leg and dragging his bad leg behind. At the sight of me he stood noticeably still.

Ellis looked older than I remembered him. His shoulders were stooped slightly, and he held himself stiffly, leaning heavily on a cane. Although he wore his customary combination of pastel-colored slacks and white shirt with a squared-off hem, he did not seem to fill his clothes so well; he seemed somehow thinner, his size not quite so imposing.

'What are you—' he began, then stopped himself, his expression surprised and a bit confused. 'I thought you were in jail.'

'I was,' I said. 'I got out this afternoon.'

He scratched his beard with his fingertips—a habitual, nervous gesture—

looked to his left, hung his cane by the curved handle from a peg on the wall.

'Have you seen your father?' he asked, looking back.

I shook my head, no.

'I came here first,' I said.

Neither of us seemed to know what to say next.

Ellis hobbled past me, behind me, to the cabinet over the shampoo sink. I heard the cabinet open, the clink of glass, the thump of a single bottle set heavily on the counter.

'Actually,' I admitted, for want of amenities, coming directly to the point, 'I was brought here: I'm supposed to find out about the agency.'

There was a long pause, a distinct hesitation before I heard the cap removed from the bottle.

I turned the barber's chair to face him.

'That's part of the deal Stacey Veldran arranged to get me released: I'm supposed to find out whether or not you're bringing in illegal aliens and putting them to work.'

He shot me a hard glance, poured the tequila, took out the triple sec.

'And I'm supposed to ask about a Panamanian named Esperoza, a banker.'

Ellis did not look at me, but said, 'I have to get a lime,' and hobbled into the back room.

Through the door I heard him open the refrigerator and poke around in it. Cans and containers slid, ringing the racklike shelves; the plastic vegetable drawer opened and closed.

Ellis appeared in the doorway, rolling the lime he had found between his palms, a hard glint in his eye.

'Most of them are just poor people from Central America,' he said. '"Illegal aliens" makes it sound like they're from another planet.'

I nodded slightly, granting him that point.

'How do you get them in?' I asked.

He held the lime up and inspected it, turning it back and forth, ignoring my question. He limped back to the small counter beside the shampoo sink and from a place I could not see took out a long-bladed knife. He sliced the lime, squeezed it into the plastic cup, added triple sec to make a room-temperature margarita, his tonic.

'Getting them in is the easy part,' he said, turning back to me, pointedly not offering me a drink. 'Why do you want to know?'

'I'm curious to know why I went to jail,' I said evenly. 'I'd like to know what I was protecting.'

He looked at me over the rim of his cup.

'You went to jail because you were stupid,' he said flatly. I expected that.

'*I* worked in good faith,' I said. 'How many sons would suspect their own father? And his brother?'

His eyes narrowed slightly in a curiously questioning way.

'You'd be better off if you knew the facts, Tony.'

'I know the facts well enough,' I replied, putting a cool, hard edge on my voice. 'Dad explained it to me after I was arrested, part of it, anyway—I guess he figured I should have something interesting to think about while I was in jail. Or maybe he figured he owed it to me since the two of you had been using me all along.' I let Ellis sit with that a moment before I went on. 'Dad goes to Central America and travels around, talking to the poor people in his fine, educated Spanish—we've both heard him when he gets started, the way his speech slows down and he seems to give you each word as if it were some precious, articulated gift. He tells them he can get them to America. If they're strong or pretty or have some special skill he arranges to bring them here. My guess is he probably just buys them new clothes and a plane ticket, since Immigration and Naturalization doesn't expect illegal aliens to have that kind of money. Maybe he gets them a green card or a tourist visa, too, but he doesn't have to be too careful about that; there's no sense wasting money: if they're caught it's no big deal. The worst the Immigration people do is send them back—and they can try again.'

I saw that Ellis was looking past me, at some point over my shoulder, so I added, 'How am I doing so far?'

His eyes came back to me, and I went on before he could say anything, 'Once they're in this country the agency finds them jobs and puts them to work. You put them to work, Ellis, and for the kindness of bringing them here and finding them jobs those *poor people* owe you so much you take a percentage of their salary for as long as they work.'

'No,' Ellis said, shaking his head, his eyes wandering again, 'not for as long as they work, only until they repay us—the same way they would have to repay any private employment agency.'

'Repay you at what interest?' I asked snidely, thinking involuntarily of Randy, of the interest *he* would have to pay.

Ellis did not reply to me but took a step to one side, lifted the hair-drying dome on a low chair, then turned and sat down heavily, bad leg straight out in front of him, good leg bent. For a moment he seemed to search his thoughts, but I recognized how he was setting the stage—trying to change the mood and the pace of the conversation by lowering himself, literally, in a calm, awkward way that drew attention to his leg—and I was ready for him.

I said, 'Now you'll tell me what a great social service you're performing, how the peasants eat garbage and live in shacks—'

He stopped me with a cutting glance and waved one arm to indicate the shop.

'Do I look like I'm making a lot of money, Tony?'

I had considered that, too. I had had a year to consider quite a few things, and Ellis and his shop had been among them: I had thought long and hard about the newspapers stacked haphazardly beside the door, about the dirty clothes thrown carelessly into the hamper with the soiled barber's towels; I had thought of Ellis asleep on the fold-out bed, his feet stuck out over the end of it, and of Ellis cooking his dinner on the hot plate that was partially hidden beneath the bedside table. And I had almost felt sorry for him until I had realized quite suddenly that that was how I was *meant* to feel, that he had subtly orchestrated his way of life to achieve that effect. Why else would he live as he did, making it appear he was poverty-stricken when I knew for a fact he was a wealthy man? Wealth brought with it a certain freedom, power over the elements of daily life, and Ellis was conducting his life as he chose.

'You like it here,' I said with certainty. 'You like the idea of people thinking of poor, lame Ellis, all alone in his rundown cottage. Poor, pitiful Ellis who never quite made it.'

His eyes were steady on mine.

'Poor, pitiful Ellis who makes so much money he needs someone to launder it.' I smiled coldly. 'Which was what I did, thinking I was simply exchanging currency.'

I pushed myself out of the chair and moved to the small counter beside the shampoo sink. I felt Ellis's watchful gaze on me as I poured myself a drink, casually mixing the tequila and the triple sec, slicing the lime. When I turned back to him I held the drink in one hand and the knife in the other, idly sighting down its long blade.

'But somewhere along the line someone screwed up, didn't they? Or maybe they got nervous about me, thinking I would realize how I had been used—I was, after all, the one link between my uncle's agency that made the money and my father's investment service that hid it. Someone thought I would see how you two were working me from both sides and try to do something about it—or maybe get a piece of the action for myself. So they put a half ton of dope in with one of my shipments not knowing I would never have figured it out, not in this lifetime. I was blinded by my own trust.' I pointed the knife at him. 'I trusted you.'

Ellis looked at the knife, then at me, holding my gaze calmly. I turned to one side and stabbed the knife into the counter. It sank deeply into the soft wood and stood there.

'Who launders the money now?' I asked coolly, turning back. 'Your little friend

Stacey Veldran? José the cane-cutter's helpful daughter?'

I took a sip of my drink and watched Ellis watching me, waiting to see if I had more to say. After a moment he looked away, interlaced his fingers, rubbed one knuckle over his lips thoughtfully.

'Why did you quit coming to see me?' he asked.

'Coming to see you when?' I answered, though I knew exactly what he meant.

He did not acknowledge my shallow evasion but again looked directly at me, his eyes very hard.

'When you were coming by regularly,' he said, 'you once asked me why your mother's death affected me so deeply. I didn't answer very well then, and I think you ought to know why—or do you think you have it figured out already?'

I stared at him coldly, feeling that peculiar hollowness that precedes anger.

'I gave your mother the polio that killed her,' he said flatly.

I felt the blood drain from my face. I did not want to hear another of his stories—I did not want to hear about my mother at all, not now—but I was too stunned to object.

'The doctors said I carried the polio with me when I went to Tegucigalpa to visit. There had been an outbreak in New Orleans. I came down with it first and gave it to her.'

Ellis looked at his bad leg and put his hand on his thigh, squeezing it tightly, kneading it.

I did not know what to say—or even if I could say anything.

'Your father will never forgive me for it. He knows it wasn't my fault, but deep down he can't help blaming me: he looks at me, and he sees her.'

Ellis stopped kneading his leg and looked back at me.

'Your father and I decided when you were very young not to tell you or your sister. There didn't seem any reason you should hate me, too.' He shortened his gaze and looked at the thick orthopedic sole of the black boot on his right foot, twisting his ankle to examine the long high heel; then he looked at the other boot and its thin sole, the two-inch difference between the length of the boots the difference in the length of his legs. 'I never parachuted out of an airplane,' he said. 'That's the story I tell because I hate the way people look at you when you say you've had polio.' He took a sip of his margarita. 'The scar on my leg is from reconstructive surgery—that's why the navy made me into a barber, because I was "unfit."'

He drank again, this time taking a long swallow and downing the margarita.

'So now you know,' he said, and pushed himself to his feet. 'You want another drink?' he asked, raising his empty cup.

I shook my head, and he walked around me. I stared blankly at the chair he had left, seeing the deep impression his weight had made on the seat, knowing what he was doing and why—and determined not to let him distract me, not this time.

'What about Esperoza?' I asked. 'Who is he?'

I looked back at Ellis in time to see him remove the knife from the counter, loosening it before pulling it free. He seemed to be thinking over how he should reply, so I added, 'No more stories, Ellis.'

He glanced at me out of the corners of his eyes, then stirred his drink with the blade of the knife, put the knife down flat, picked up the drink, and looked down into it, seeming to study it.

'In Panama,' he began, measuring his words carefully 'Señor Esperoza is a very powerful man. He's head of the commission that regulates all Panamanian banks.' Ellis looked up and turned to face me. 'According to him, the United States applied pressure to get him appointed so he could change the way the banking laws are enforced, particularly the secrecy laws that make it so easy to hide money there.'

Ellis shrugged.

'Señor Esperoza knows that any changes he makes will affect some other very powerful people adversely, and he's afraid harm will come to his family. He came to see me and asked if I could get his sons out of the country. It was difficult to arrange because they had to be smuggled *out* of Panama as well as *into* this country.'

I did not ask Ellis why he would enter into such a risky venture as I knew full well the extraordinary bank secrecy laws in Panama—and the favors a powerful Panamanian banker could do for him.

'I made the arrangements,' Ellis continued, 'but somewhere along the line, I seem to have misplaced his sons.'

'How do you misplace someone's sons?' I asked curiously.

Ellis scraped his thumbnail over the ounce markings on the side of the plastic cup.

'It's easier than you might think,' he replied.

I shook my head slowly.

'You have no idea where they are?'

'I only know where they *aren't*: they aren't in Panama. And I only know that because Señor Esperoza is here in New Orleans looking for them. He came to see me yesterday.'

'And?' I pressed, seeing that Ellis was thinking again, his eyes flicking about.

'And so I sent Stacey to see if she could make a deal to get you out of jail so you could help me find them.'

Ellis raised the mixing cup to his lips and

drank too quickly, forgetful of having refilled his drink. Some of the margarita spilled; he wiped at his chin irritably.

'If I don't deliver his two sons to him within three days, Señor Esperoza told me that he will *disappear* members of my family.'

'That's nice,' I said sourly, then asked, 'What does that mean, *disappear*?'

'It means, Tony, that if we don't find the two boys and get them back, Señor Esperoza has threatened to take us one at a time to remote spots and kill us.' Ellis scratched his beard. 'But we still have two more days,' he added.

'That's nice,' I said again.

CHAPTER FIVE

I had kept my apartment simply by paying for it. On the first day of each month, as faithfully—and as symbolically—as other prisoners had scratched through calendars to mark the time, I had written checks against my brokerage account for rent, phone, and utilities, carefully subtracting the amounts from my balance before adding in my dividends. And from Ellis's shop in the Faubourg Marigny I went there, walking slowly into the French Quarter on Decatur Street, passing the French Market, the shops and restaurants, the Café du Monde, Jackson Square, noticing details: the way the buildings butted one up against another, how steel rods on edge supported the ornate balconies, plaster crumbling over brick.

My wife and I had found the apartment five years before; we had furnished it piece by piece in the three years before her accident. And although it was too big for me by myself, after her death I had stayed on in it because I had never been able to summon the energy necessary to undo what we had done together, to dismantle the only evidence of the time we had spent together.

My wife was a biologist, and one warm Saturday afternoon, when I was napping in our bedroom, she and her assistant had been using a seine—a large net with sinkers on one end and floats on the other—to sample the fish population in a small bay into which a paper company was dumping its chemical waste. She became entangled in the net, her waders filled with water, she panicked and went under before her assistant could cut her free. She drowned in four feet of water, and I remembered thinking, when awakened from my nap with the news of her death, *This is important. This changes my life forever.* But at the time I could find no significance to it, no meaning, just as now my new freedom did not seem as momentous as it should. Instead, I found myself wondering if there was actually a Panamanian banker who intended to *disappear* me. I wondered if Ellis had really carried the polio that had killed my mother, and as I approached the door to my apartment, I wondered if the lock had been changed in the year since I had used my key.

I remembered to pull the key out just a hair and to jiggle it as I turned it; the lock clicked open with a familiar sound. I went into the damp courtyard that smelled of cats and climbed the corkscrewlike staircase with the worn wooden stairs that sagged tiredly. At my door I hesitated, wondering what I would do if, when I opened it, my wife came charging out of the bedroom as she used to, sliding across the polished wood floor in her oversized moose-skin slippers, arms out wide for a hug, smiling broadly, exclaiming, 'Curbelo!' like some good-natured war cry; but it was quiet inside, a bit musty but otherwise just as I had left it.

In the living room I opened the two uncurtained casement windows and turned the air-conditioning on high. In the bedroom I saw the huge bed was unmade and rumpled. On the floor was a pair of sneakers. Canted precariously against the wall was a bottle of Russian vodka. I picked up the vodka and eyed it speculatively, sloshing the clear liquid around the bottom, carrying it with me into the bathroom.

Around its margin the full-length bathroom

mirror was both beveled and mottled, giving to the reflections it cast a certain dated quality that the claw-foot bathtub and white tile wainscot reinforced. I set the bottle of vodka on the floor and turned on the water in the tub, adjusting it to run very hot. Idly waiting for the tub to fill I wandered back into the bedroom and undressed, throwing my clothes on the bed, then taking my tie to the closet to hang it. On the inside of the closet door I saw my diplomas, one above the other, right there where I had tacked them beneath the shoe rack that hung from the top of the door. My first degree, a bachelor's in economics, was concealed behind tennis shoes and loafers; my second, a master's of business administration, was covered by the lace-up wingtips and plain-toed shoes I usually wore with suits. I smiled slightly, remembering that I had taken the diplomas out of the folders in which they had been awarded and had hung them there at my wife's insistence that I hang them *somewhere*—and even she had smiled at my choice of places. I rubbed my neck and looped the tie over the doorknob.

The water in the tub was so hot steam floated from the surface; the mirror had clouded and the air was thick and warm. I stretched out until only my nose was out of the water, sitting up occasionally to grab the bottle of vodka as it floated past, sipping from it and feeling its burn as I slid back down, eyes closed, listening to my heart's dull thumping.

Not too bad, I thought contentedly. *There are moments when this life is not too bad.*

Without opening my eyes I raised one foot out of the water and groped lazily for the porcelain knob on the hot water faucet. I felt a hard double tap on the back of my foot and opened my eyes, startled to see a man in a suit sitting on the edge of the tub, poised there, one hand in his lap, a long-barreled revolver in his other hand, just above the water.

'You will stand up, please,' he said, and I did, feeling too rubbery to be frightened but moving very slowly and very deliberately, looking at him.

He was a small man, slender and compact, with dark brown eyes the color of strong tea. His forehead sloped back to his wavy brown hair, and his complexion was handsomely dark but pocked with scars in the hollows of his cheeks. He seemed somehow reluctant to point the revolver at me; as I stood up, he did, too, but he kept the barrel down, pointed at the water somewhere near my feet.

'Señor Esperoza would like to see you,' he said, looking at me, holding my gaze.

I nodded, and his eyes left me. He turned slightly, reaching with his free hand toward the towel rack, and with both hands I grabbed his forearm, yanking it down, slamming his wrist against the rounded steel edge of the tub. The revolver came loose, dangling now in his fingertips. I slammed his wrist again. The revolver splashed near my feet. I dropped to my knees; immediately he was on my back, pushing me face down into the water. The revolver was between my calves. His arm was around my neck, choking me; his full weight was on my back, holding me under. With one convulsive jerk I brought up my knees, pulling them forward painfully as I pressed down against the bottom of the tub. My head cracked against the spigot. I grabbed for the revolver and got it, then yelled, loudly, as I aimed it at the side of the tub and pulled the trigger. The water erupted with a huge concussing-ringing force, a stunningly brutal slap. He fell out of the tub, both hands over his ears, and I fell back, mouth open, staring vacantly, rolling my eyes slowly, trying to make them focus, seeing then the second man, no taller than the first but much broader, compact but very solid. I threw one hand up weakly, a gesture of surrender, but he stepped over the man on the floor, his eyes fixed on my face, moving toward me with purpose, a short, dull silver baseball bat clutched chest high; then behind the man approaching there was a third man, a black man who towered over him. The black man grabbed the baseball bat with one big hand, and when the solid man turned, surprised, in two extraordinarily rapid movements the black man hit him, his big fist catching him first on the cheek, then on the temple, with such force the man slammed against the wall and bounced, knees buckling, held up now only by the black man's hand around his throat.

The black man held up the baseball bat, looked at it, and sneered derisively.

He said, 'Motherfucker uses an *aluminum* baseball bat? Shit. He think he playing softball?' Then he looked at me, and added, 'You clean enough. Get out the tub.'

My ears rang fiercely, and my head ached where I had cracked it against the spigot; I stood up uncertainly, holding on to both sides of the tub.

Still clutching the solid man by the throat, the black man reached down and pulled the plug, checked to see that the water was draining, flicked the water from his hand.

Dazed by the shot's concussing force, I watched him, blinking, trying to see more clearly.

He was thick in the chest and shoulders and thick in the neck. His nose was flat, the nostrils flared into round, black holes. Sheer size gave him a presence that filled the room, but he moved effortlessly, gracefully, without any of the clumsiness I usually observed in men his size. His sloe eyes, set close together and half-closed assessingly, moved over me, then landed on the mark the bullet had made in the side of the tub.

I reached down and ran my finger over the deep dent, surprised to find that the peanut-sized hollow was very smooth, as if the steel beneath the enamel had been polished rather than struck.

I saw him watching me impatiently, so I stood up straight and reached for a towel.

As I stepped uncertainly out of the tub he lifted the solid man into it, rolled him so that he floated face up in the draining water, and felt his pockets by patting them. He picked up the revolver, then turned and picked up the second man, too, and put him on top of the first, watching them both, seeing them flail about to breathe. He bent from the waist and put his fist down low, one long black finger sticking out of it.

'You little fuckers get out the tub I break your skinny backs,' he said, the words spaced apart and distinct; and he held his arm like that, bent at the elbow as he stood up straight and aimed the pointed finger at me. 'You and me going to talk,' he said.

I put my palms over my ears and pressed in and out as I moved my jaw, trying to stop the ringing in my ears.

The black man looked again at the mark the bullet had made, shook his head slowly, turned, and went out of the bathroom.

The bottle of vodka had remained unbroken. I toweled myself off, wrapped the towel around my middle, retrieved the bottle from the corner of the tub, and followed him into the bedroom, now fairly certain there was someone who intended to *disappear* me—and more than a little curious to know why the black man had prevented it.

He positioned himself on the corner of the bed, leaning back on one elbow, so that he could see into the bathroom; and as I walked out he kept his gaze on the tub.

He said, 'How'd you know that gun would work underwater?'

'I didn't,' I replied. I put my finger in my ear and wiggled it. 'At the moment I'm not sure I'm so happy it did.'

He looked at me out of the corners of his eyes, sat up, and unloaded the revolver, then tossed it onto the middle of the bed. He crossed his long legs as he turned to face me, shaking the bullets like lucky dice in his hand.

'Who are you?' I asked.

He did not reply right away but looked over his shoulder into the bathroom. I noticed then that his suit was gray with thin black vertical stripes woven into it, an unusual material I had never seen before. Beneath the suit he wore a black shirt with gray stripes and two heavy gold necklaces, one tight around his big neck, the other dangling loosely against the dark skin on his chest.

'You heard of a dude named Lionel Day?'

he asked, ignoring my question but looking back at me, apparently satisfied with what he had seen in the bathroom. 'He's called Lips.'

I shook my head, no.

'He was a classmate of yours.'

'He went to Tulane?' I asked curiously.

He gave me a pained, sour look.

'Motherfucker was in jail.'

I shook my head again.

'Don't matter,' he said. 'I find that nigger myself.'

From the way he said it, his brown-black eyes dead serious and determined, I was sure he would find him, and just for a moment, looking at the size of him, every part of him brutally big and powerful, I felt sorry for Lionel Day, Lips—whoever he was.

'My name is DeLloyd Lincoln,' he finally said. 'I work for your uncle—used to, anyway. Me and Stacey worked together, making collections for the agency.'

'You mind if I get dressed?' I asked.

DeLloyd again looked over his shoulder, glancing into the bathroom.

'Pack a bag, too,' he advised. 'If you smart, you be gone from here a while.'

I opened the top drawer of my dresser and found my shorts and socks just as I had left them, jumbled together, unsorted.

'What are you doing here?' I asked, not looking up, rummaging through the drawer but listening carefully.

'Stacey tell me you the man's nephew and you gettin' out of jail. I come to see you—I figure you should hear my side, too, since they tryin' to lay all this sorry shit off on me. And I figure maybe you know something about Lips—maybe heard something inside—so I parked across the street when I see you come in. I see those two behind you'—he flipped his wrist, jerking his thumb at the bathroom—'one of them trying to be cool with his baseball bat, holding it up along his leg. I figure it time to come in.'

'You figured right,' I said, slipping on a pair of shorts and pulling them up.

'They just smoke,' he said, and again flipped his thumb toward the bathroom, casually dismissing the two men in the tub.

I glanced at him as I moved to the closet, but he was looking down, shaking the bullets in his hand, distracted or thoughtful, it was hard to tell which.

'First I figure, shit, it's his money. Give me my sweetness, I make any kind of righteous deal he want. Then the shit get heavy, I think: a man don't float his own money. What for? He wait and invest it if it his—buy a treasury bill or some other good shit. But by then Lips gone rabbit, leave me with the whole thing. I here looking like every kind of fool. I break Lips's nappy head I find him.'

I zipped up the trousers I had put on as he spoke.

'What are you talking about?' I asked.

He shot me a withering glance.

'The collections, man. The collections and your uncle. Ain't nobody told you nothing?'

'I just got out of jail, pal.'

'Maybe you just got full of shit,' he said, glaring at me.

There was something in his eyes that reminded me of the way Stacey Veldran had looked at me that morning: the combination of resentment, anger, and something else that was deeper, something near hatred.

'Why don't you run it down to me?' I suggested.

De Lloyd dropped his glance and looked glumly at the revolver lying where he had tossed it on the bed, cylinder open, long barrel pointing at the disarrayed pillows. He dropped the bullets near the revolver and poked at them, pushing the shiny silver cartridges into a row. He picked up the empty casing and held it between two fingers, turning it.

'I meet your uncle,' he began, 'I parking cars in the Monteleone garage, hustling my ass for tips, running after Cadillacs and Mercedes, doing everything but tap dancing for the pinch-faced bitches. Man give me a quarter he careful-like, dropping it onto my palm so he won't have to touch my hand, like he might catch something—maybe be a nigger himself. Women, shit, they worse:

don't want to even *see* me.'

DeLloyd flipped the empty shell casing at the wall, watched it bounce and hit the floor.

'I bring your uncle his raggedy old car, he cool, talk sometimes. He say come see him, maybe he got a job for me pays better than parking cars. He say it two or three times I pass by his beauty parlor; I think, shit, this motherfucker working a number on me, live like he on welfare and offering me a job.'

DeLloyd picked up a live round and etched its soft lead nose with his thumbnail, holding it upright and flicking his nail across it, as if he were striking a match.

'First thing that old man does, he cut my hair.'

I smiled to myself thinking of that scene: DeLloyd in the red vinyl barber's chair, looking around casually, wondering just what he had wandered into; and Ellis behind him, scissors in hand, tonic on the shampoo shelf, hobbling from one side of the chair to the other, explaining nothing but excitedly telling some outrageous story before at last he came to the point.

'I'm thinking this old motherfucker ain't got two nickels to rub together and he tell me he got an employment agency. He say the agency send people around for jobs, and I supposed to believe he got the jobs, too: he say he got a car wash, a yard service, a fast-chicken place, a motel—shit, he say he got everything except a motherfucking bank. He say he need a man to pick up money and that man get to keep five percent of what he pick up. I say, shit.'

'Why you?' I interrupted. 'Why didn't he get someone he knew?'

'Just for that, so no one know the pickup man. They wonder who he is—and if he black besides, big and black even better—they won't get too cozy with him and think about holding back his money.'

I found a shirt in the second drawer of the dresser, unfolded it, and put it on, buttoning it slowly.

'So you took the job?'

'Man, I didn't take nothing. I said, this I got to see: this old man really need somebody to pick up cash receipts, I kiss his ass on Bourbon and Canal.'

DeLloyd looked up, watched me work a button, looked directly at me.

'First month my five percent come to over three thousand dollars.'

I thought about that for a moment, multiplying it out, then whistled softly.

'You right about that,' DeLloyd added. 'That old man make money when he fart.'

I finished buttoning my shirt and turned to look out the window, feeling a faint disgust, wondering how much Ellis made his clients pay, those *poor people* from Central America; and wondering what he did with all that money, how he used it.

On the roof terrace one floor below, my neighbor was watering the bushy plants that lined her parapet. At each plant she tipped a galvanized watering can, moved the fine, showerlike stream of water in a circle, then lowered the can while with her free hand she fluffed the leaves and ruffled them. Water had soaked through the front of her blouse and made it transparent. I saw her breasts moving fluidly, her tight brown nipples brushing the long green leaves.

I knew that her name was Margaret but that she liked to be called just plain Marge; and I knew that she was a secretary in the international department of the bank I had used when I was trading currency. I had met her there, and when she had asked me to keep an eye out for an apartment she might buy, I had suggested the one she was in now, which then had been vacant for some time. My knowledge of her seemed to come from a long time before, across an expanse of time much greater than the number of days would indicate, and when, feeling my glance, she looked up curiously, I stepped away from the window, not quite ready to confront so casually the time that had intervened.

I turned back to DeLloyd, and said, 'Did you kiss his ass on Bourbon and Canal?'

DeLloyd did not seem amused by my question. I tucked in my shirttail and went back to the closet to get a tie.

'So where's the problem?' I added, jerking my head to indicate the men in the tub. 'Those two?'

DeLloyd was watching me, waiting for me to turn to face him. When I did, he said, 'You think you a cute motherfucker? Think you want to fuck with me for fun?'

I looked down at the tie I had chosen, gray stripes over dark red.

'Sorry,' I said, meaning it, knowing he was right to upbraid me.

He stood up in one smooth motion, adjusted his coat by rolling his broad shoulders, stepped into the bathroom. After a moment he stepped back out and leaned against the doorjamb, his hands in his pockets, his eyes hard but troubled, as if he were making a very difficult decision.

'Stacey told me something wrong with you,' he said, 'can't be serious, think you so smart. I tell her, man just did a year in jail; it change a man, make him so he don't know how to act. She say, man never knew: man never been on the street, never had to hustle his ass, wonder how he going to eat. She say, that's what wrong with the man.'

DeLloyd paused.

I started to say something, thought better of it, waited for him to continue.

He took his hands out of his pockets and crossed his arms on his chest, his decision apparently made but his eyes still troubled.

'Your uncle always owed money somewhere,' he said finally, 'so me and Stacey always out chasing after it. Supposed to be, she keep watch on me; I keep a watch on her. But it take time to collect the money—sometimes you get to talk to the people, let them know you serious, let them know they going to pay, one way or the other.'

One way or the other, I thought, looking at DeLloyd, at the ominous size of him, and recalling the extraordinary quickness and power he had displayed, his facility for violence.

'So we run behind sometimes. Had to. We just collectin' the money; we ain't makin' it. Your uncle got no problem with that. He know. He used to make the collections himself—probably still could he had to, big like he is—but he gettin' old.'

I wrapped my tie around my fingers, looking at it but thinking of Ellis, remembering the one time he had hit me, how he had slapped me on the back of the head, hard, and how it had stung as he held me in the barber's chair, glaring down at me, towering over me.

'Sometimes we see something good,' DeLloyd continued, 'we slow on purpose: we use the money before we hand it in. Your uncle know that, too.'

'Use the money how?' I asked cautiously.

'We make deals,' DeLloyd replied, shrugging the deals off as unimportant but doing it in an overstressed way, jerking his shoulder forward and back, going on too quickly. 'Everybody make a little something extra, everybody happy. Problem is, we got a deal look like it's going bad. Now everybody out trying to cover their own ass, trying to put it off on somebody else. Problem is, I got to find Lips to see what the problem is, and they in the way.' He jerked his thumb over his shoulder, pointing through the open door into the bathroom.

I put my tie around my neck and began to adjust it under my collar.

'I don't understand,' I said.

DeLloyd pushed himself away from the doorjamb and stood up straight, dropping his hands to his sides as he took an agitated step forward.

'Somebody running a game,' he said. 'They see the deal go bad they figure they got to cover it, throw up smoke. They see the man's sons coming through they grab 'em, figure nobody worry about money when the man's sons missing.'

'Esperoza's sons?' I asked. 'You think somebody grabbed Esperoza's sons to draw attention away from the deal?'

'Think, shit. I know.'

DeLloyd stepped in close to me, pressing.

'And they goin' to say it's me that did it.'

I caught his hot gaze and held it, looking up at him.

'Did you?' I asked evenly.

'Shit, man, that's what I telling you,' he said, his words gaining emphasis from his massive, threatening nearness. 'Only one I know for sure ain't did it is me.'

I accepted that and stepped away from him with relief, turning again to face the window. On the terrace below Marge was inspecting a single plant closely, holding several leaves in one hand and leaning toward them, frowning.

Behind me, DeLloyd said, 'I here so you know my side, show you I ain't hidin' nothing before you start pokin' around.'

Marge looked up and saw me before I could step back.

'I here to warn you, too,' DeLloyd went on. 'You in a tight place, my friend. Those little fuckers serious about you disappearin'.'

Marge smiled perkily, and said, 'No kidding! Tony Curbel! Welcome home!'

DeLloyd added, his voice surprisingly gentle, 'You try to hide, they get your family. What I heard, they just got your father.'

CHAPTER SIX

Three blocks from my apartment was a barroom I had frequented. At the bar the regular clientele was largely local, and the waiters and waitresses, off-duty bartenders, cooks, limousine drivers, hotel portrait-painters, and on-call plumbers generally knew each other, if not by name, enough to nod acquaintance. As a rule it was a friendly sort of group, gregarious, hard-drinking, indulgent, and self-indulgent short of rowdy—the sort of group that would readily understand a four-day binge but would never tolerate a crying drunk; the sort of group that would discuss sports with more fervor than politics and would spend a large percentage of their disposable incomes on liquor and bets with their bookies.

In jail late at night I had often imagined that barroom, picturing the dim yellow lights, the heavy oak barstools, the cypress barge-board walls decorated with maps of various places. I had pictured the small map of the state that hung between the double doors that opened out onto the street; the long map of the Mississippi River that stretched behind the worn bar, behind the rows of bottles. Some of the maps were old and faded, marked and re-marked along the routes of journeys made or planned by anonymous or imaginary travelers. I had considered myself a regular in the bar, though I knew deep down I was an impostor, a pretender to the spirit of sports, bets, and errant journeys. But the image of it had seemed somehow important to me in jail because I had known with certainty that it was there, ongoing; and because I had known it would be there still, unchanged, when I got out.

DeLloyd had used two of my neckties to tie the hands of the men in the tub. I had heard him warning them as he knotted the ties, telling them how long they should wait before they moved, how lucky they were that he was in such good humor.

I had packed my briefcase with a change of clothes and a razor.

On the way out of my apartment DeLloyd had stopped to write down three telephone numbers for me—his, Stacey Veldran's, the agency's answering service—but then he had seemed reluctant to give the numbers to me. He had folded the sheet of paper on which he had written and creased it, angrily, it seemed, pinching the edge of the paper between thumb and first finger, before he had extended it hesitantly, his lips pressed tightly together. And it was only after he had gone, driving away quickly in his expensive German car, that I had unfolded the sheet and realized he had not been reluctant to give me the numbers; rather, he had been reluctant to let me see his handwriting, a labored, unpracticed, barely legible scrawl. And as I had walked away, drawn to the barroom I had imagined so often, I recalled the way he had held the pen, his big hand wrapped around it clumsily, self-consciously, so painfully different from the grace and confidence of his other movements.

The barmaid said in a friendly way, 'Where have you been, stranger?'

'Passing time,' I replied evasively. 'Trying to get by.'

'Is there any other way?' she said, and wiped the bar in front of me. 'What'll you have today?'

I ordered Scotch with a splash of soda.

It was after five o'clock. I knew my father's office would be closed; so when I asked for change to use the pay phone it was to try to call him at home. I knew I had to call—if only to know that I had tried—but I hesitated, sipping my drink, feeling the first sip bite and the second sip go down smoothly.

DeLloyd could be lying, I thought, *and my father at that moment was on his way home from work. And even if he does not answer at home that does not mean that Esperoza has him. He travels frequently. Sometimes he goes out after work or works outside in his garden.*

Some garden, I thought, seeing my father,

hoe in hand, vigorously chopping at the dirt, his face red and flushed, sweat dripping from his nose—and thinking, too, that I was as ashamed to call him as I was fearful that he would not be there. I was afraid of what he would say to me, afraid to hear the scorn in his voice.

I tapped a quarter against the bar, went to the pay phone, and dialed it, knowing by the familiar sound of the tones that I had dialed correctly. I let the phone ring thirteen times before I hung up, deciding to try again in a few minutes. I went back to my place at the bar, picked up my drink, studied the sweat that had formed on the side of the glass, feeling the dampness on my palms.

'*Yo soy Curbelo*,' I said to myself, raising the glass to my lips, thinking just then of my grandmother, the soft sound of her voice, her calm, dark eyes. I wondered how she would advise me to deal with the dread I felt, the dread and the fear intermixed.

'You must think of the good things,' she had once told me, 'and deal with the bad as it comes.'

And I wondered if that was what she had advised my father when he had been forced to leave Mochita, dispossessed, and during the frightful years that followed: when back from the war he had found that his brother had advanced, in comfort, much further than he; when his wife had died and left him with two small children; when money had been a constant, threatening problem. I wondered if she had understood my father's bitterness, if she had seen the anger grow in him until it ran just beneath the surface, just beneath his mask of cool civility.

Think of the good things, I thought, and I did.

I remembered how my father had taught me to throw a baseball, patiently explaining how to grip the seams and practicing with me, day after day. I remembered the nights he had let me stay up late, to be with him, and the day he had taken me to his office and had shown me around, proudly introducing me as his son, his 'junior partner.' But those memories brought with them an emotional content that summoned up the boy in me, the boy who had needed to love his father—needed to love him doubly, enough for both father and mother—yet who so often had dreaded his father's approach because the anger was there, erupting through his cool civility in uncontrollable, devastating furies. That boy remembered too well the turkey thrown down so hard the gravy had splashed to the dining room ceiling. He remembered the sting of his father's slaps, the toys assaulted and brutally kicked to splinters, the screaming sound of his father's heavy belt and the firelike pain when it struck. Through the mitigating thoughts I had rehearsed so often—through all my *reasons* and recollections of the good things—that fear and dread was in me now, as alive, if not as powerful, as it had ever been.

I put my drink down on the bar, folded a paper napkin into quarters, wiped my hands, knowing there was more to it, too, a much more substantial fear. That fear had begun the day after I had been arrested, when my father had come to see me.

Heedless of the way I had looked, unshaven and filthy, badly shaken by the night I had spent in jail, after my release on bail I had gone directly to my office, taking a cab from Central Lock-up, and once at my desk I had begun to review my files, taking out the documents I needed, preparing my defense. As I had made a new file, placing the correspondence and the receipts in order, anger had transformed first to relieved confidence, then to outrage: my role as broker was unequivocally clear. What had been bought with Honduran lempiras had very obviously been intended to be sold for U.S. dollars, the exchange efficiently made. On behalf of my client I had bought the lumber, paid the taxes, arranged the shipping, the insurance, the sale on my end—and that was all. I knew nothing about the half ton of marijuana that had been found. No court could convict me. So when my father had appeared I had been glad to see him and had rushed through my explanation excitedly, showing him my file, pacing back and forth, pausing to scratch hasty notes on my pad.

He had stopped me with a glance, a strangely sad glance that had become very hard as he had begun to speak, ordering me to plead guilty to the charges the police had made because, he explained, the money I had thought I was in good faith exchanging for a Honduran businessman was, in fact, Curbelo money—just as a substantial portion of the money I had exchanged in the previous years was, in fact, Curbelo money.

'We,' he had said, 'we as a family cannot risk the investigation a trial would bring. We cannot risk either the money or our good name.'

At first I had been stunned, unable to believe what he was saying. For years, many of my clients had not been clients at all but fronts for my own family's business. Then I had seen in his sad-hard expression the truth of it, and I had felt a righteous fury rise.

'*No iré a la cárcel*,' I had protested vehemently, sweeping my desk clean, scattering papers across the floor. 'I will not go to jail.'

'You will do what you have to do,' he had replied harshly, tearing my new file in half. 'You are a Curbel.'

I could not believe it. No father would send his own son to jail, not for money.

Sitting there on that barstool, idly wiping the bar with the napkin I had folded, even after a year in jail, still I could not believe it. Throughout my life my father had been there for me. He had been my security, my solid anchor in the winds and tides of events *out there*, away from home, where people died. Whatever his faults I had needed him and loved him, and I believed that in his own way, as well as he knew how, he had loved me, too. Consistently. Unfailingly. As neither my mother nor my wife had been able.

I threw the napkin at the trashcan and went back to the pay phone. Again he did not answer.

I felt my own anger rise, the fear and the dread transforming, becoming a cold, determined fury. I knew only one place to begin: I called Skinny and arranged to meet him.

CHAPTER SEVEN

Very suddenly a cool breeze came in from the south. The wind did not gust but blew steadily, and it was charged with energy, heavy with moisture. When the first drops of rain spattered on the sidewalk, I knew I had to find cover quickly, before the downpour.

On the next corner there was another bar,

but I knew if I went in I would be trapped there by the rain; so I passed the corner and turned right, toward the river, quick-stepping to the French Market, reaching it just as the rain began in its tropical way, breaking suddenly, coming down at full force without crescendo, so heavy even the buildings across the street were obscured.

The French Market was nothing more than a loading dock, a block-long raised strip of concrete three steps high. A slightly pitched roof covered the dock itself and extended out past it, providing protection for the farmers and vendors who backed their trucks into the bays, off-loaded produce, and set up booths right there, at the back of the trucks; then they set up webbed chairs, checkerboards on card tables, and were ready for the slow evening, a friendly game, the occasional customer who wandered through.

As I stood at one end of the market, brushing the rain that had hit me from my coat, Skinny appeared, ducking between two trucks onto the walkway.

Skinny wiped the rain off his bare arms, then looked about. When he spotted me he raised one hand—more a gesture of intent than a greeting—and started toward me. His long legs kicked out, overextended, and his long arms flapped at his sides. His brown hair was wet and matted, flung straight back from his forehead.

‘Hey, Curbel,’ Skinny said when he got near. He ran both hands through his hair, then wiped them on his sleeveless green fatigue jacket. ‘Nice night.’ His eyes flicked with distaste to a nearby display of turnip greens. ‘Nice place, too,’ he said sourly. ‘Skinny can buy fruit. Why didn’t you stop at the bar? Skinny could use a beer.’

I did not reply but looked at him coolly.

‘Skinny was right behind you,’ he went on. ‘He wanted to be sure you were by yourself.’

He pulled down the zipper on his field jacket and scratched his ribs, lifting his elbow away from his body as he did so.

‘So Skinny’s here, Curbel. What do you want? Skinny’s in a hurry.’

When Skinny pulled his zipper back up it snagged momentarily and his jacket flared open; strapped across his chest I saw a black nylon holster and the butt of a long, silver revolver.

‘Did Stacey Veldran tell you anything more about the banker?’ I asked. ‘About Esperoza?’

Skinny shook his head.

‘She didn’t tell Skinny about him in the first place,’ he said. ‘She told you—Skinny only knows about him at all because he was in the next room, listening through the peephole.’ He looked away from me, then back, unabashed. ‘What about him?’

‘Did she mention a man named DeLloyd

Lincoln?' I asked, and I saw immediately that she had: it was in his eyes, a quick, feral spark of interest.

'Then you know about Lips, too,' I concluded. 'Lionel Day.'

From a display near at hand Skinny picked up a bright red creole tomato and squeezed it speculatively, testing its ripeness.

'Skinny knows about Lips and DeLloyd,' he said. 'He didn't know about your father until this afternoon.'

'You knew?' I asked dumbly, feeling the blood rise to my cheeks, knowing at once that he had withheld the information to keep me working as he directed, holding back, hoping to use the knowledge against me.

'Look on the up side, Curbel,' he said, his eyes on the tomato he held. He took a quick bite of it, put it back in the display, bite side down, wiped his mouth with the back of his hand. 'If Skinny had found out earlier, you might still be in jail—Skinny might have decided to spare you all the emotional upset.'

I stepped in close to him, close enough to smell the tomato on his breath.

'You can always go back,' he added coldly, his lips sliding off his protruding front teeth. 'That's up to you.'

I grabbed his arm, hard, and held it.

'You bastard,' I said, feeling as much as hearing the snarling edge on my words, the hot anger.

Skinny looked coolly at my hand on his arm, then shifted his shrewd, hard eyes to my face.

'So you want to dance with Skinny,' he said evenly, 'or you want to find your father?'

For a moment we stood like that, eyes locked.

'You bastard,' I said again, but softer this time, not so vehemently. I knew he was right. My anger was misdirected—Lips, DeLloyd, my father, they were all interrelated.

I released his arm, pushing him away from me as I did so.

Skinny unconcernedly licked his lips, dug into the pocket of his jeans, came out with a nickel and two pennies. He seemed to weigh the worth of the coins against the worth of his bite of tomato, shrugged, dropped the coins into the open cigar box beside the display.

'So,' he asked casually, turning back to me, 'what did your uncle have to say?'

I made a careless gesture, waving one hand disgustedly.

'He didn't say anything about Lips or DeLloyd,' I replied.

'It figures that he wouldn't,' Skinny said. He wiped at the juice that had run down his receding chin before he saw my questioning look. 'Think, Curbel,' he added, and tapped his forefinger rudely against his temple. 'Why *wouldn't* he mention them?'

'I don't know,' I said, then asked

pointedly, 'Why didn't you?'

'Your uncle didn't say anything, Curbel, because he's in on the deal. He has to be. That's the only way it figures. Why else would he let the money come in late?'

I thought about that for a moment, choosing not to consider the implications.

'Skinny's been doing his homework,' he said, smiling in a coy, self-satisfied way. 'He *knows*.'

I started to say something but waited, watching as he suddenly stepped down from the loading dock and rinsed his hands in the water pouring off the roof.

'Lips was arrested for aggravated rape six weeks ago,' he said finally, over his shoulder. 'Ten days later they turned him loose on a hundred-fifty-thousand-dollar bond. His court date was last week, but surprise, the dumb bastard never showed—the bondsman is, to say the least, a little fired up.'

Don't you know, I thought, involuntarily remembering the one bail bondsman I had ever met, the way he had licked his fat forefinger as he counted my money, his lips moving as he counted, his breath making a soft, reverent, wheezing sound, in and out.

Skinny jumped up on the walkway beside me.

'Take a walk, Curbel,' he said, and abruptly set off down the market, his long legs kicking out, farmerlike, as if stepping over furrows. After a few steps he sensed that I wasn't following, and he turned back. 'Something the matter with your feet?' he asked.

I shrugged and started walking slowly, sauntering, feeling that Skinny was moving too quickly deliberately, trying to draw me along in his high-speed wake.

He flapped his elbows impatiently.

'You want to meet Lips or what?' he said.

'Meet him?' I asked, puzzled.

'Skinny has him, man,' he said, raising his voice, exaggerating his rude nasal twang. 'Skinny has him. He's in the trunk of Skinny's car.'

He waved his loose-jointed arms excitedly.

'See, Curbel, Skinny's better to you than you think.'

* * *

We walked the length of the French Market, passing the displays of fresh fruit and vegetables, which, even in the dim light from the bare bulbs overhead, appeared tantalizingly bright in color and ripe, ready to eat. The damp air was heavy with the smell of the produce, musty but richly fertile.

Skinny had parked his old Ford between two trucks, backing it into the narrow space between them so that the trunk was in, toward the loading dock and under cover.

The rain poured from the roof and made a wet drumming sound on the hood of the car. Skinny took out his keys and popped the trunk proudly, smiling; I looked down and saw a wiry black man lying there, looking up, blinking in the light. His feet were shackled together, and his hands were cuffed, one hand on either side of the spare tire so that he had to rest his head on the sidewall. His shirt was unbuttoned, exposing his lean dark torso, and his pants were loose, so low on his narrow hips the top of his striped boxer shorts fluffed out over his belt. There was anger in the man's eyes, anger mixed with fear.

'He was easy,' Skinny said loudly, as if he were in a trophy room, boasting about a particularly handsome head. 'He went to visit his momma in the Villa d'Âmes Housing Project. Skinny kicked the door, and there he was, sitting at the table eating red beans. Skinny was so fast he didn't even try to rabbit—Skinny even pulled up a chair and ate a plate of beans.'

Skinny smiled again, looked over his shoulder as if he had just thought of something, stepped to a nearby table and picked up two ears of corn. He dropped the corn into the trunk and slammed the lid.

'He might be getting hungry,' he explained. 'He's been in there a while.'

'Hey, son of a bitch,' a loud voice called, angry.

Skinny turned so quickly it startled me. I heard the ripping sound of a zipper yanked open and saw the long silver revolver flash in his hand. He crouched as he turned, bringing his hands together, then up.

The voice belonged to a short, heavyset man who sat at a table down the walk.

'You take the corn, you pay for it,' the man said, glaring at us; then he said gruffly to the old black man who was sitting with him at the table, 'You better get down there.'

The old man stood up slowly, reluctantly, looking at the checkerboard on the table and jumping a red piece before he started toward us.

'Shit,' Skinny said softly but emphatically. He stood up straight and returned the revolver to the holster on his chest. 'See what happens when you're a nice guy?' he said, and rapped his knuckles on the trunk.

I watched the old man approach, walking stiffly, took out a dollar, and gave it to him.

He took it and put it into his pocket, shuffled back to his game.

Skinny said, 'For two ears of corn you gave him a *dollar*?'

I nodded toward the car.

'Can he breathe in there? In the trunk?'

Skinny looked at the car.

'He's all right,' he said, his expression momentarily blank and unformed. Then he recovered with a start, and said, 'Oh, yeah,' flashing a smile that faded quickly. 'Skinny was at the table eating beans.'

He looked to see if I was with him, saw that I was, leaned back against the car.

'And he's thinking: Lips is worth fifteen thousand back at the bondsman's, right? That's the ten percent he put up for his bail. When a guy's overdue the bondsman pays it, no question, so he won't have to put up the other ninetyper cent of the bail he's guaranteed if he can't produce his client. So Skinny tells Lips, man, you come up with better than the fifteen thousand you're worth from the bondsman, and Skinny'll forget he ever saw you. And it worked. Bigtime. Lips had such a line with him Skinny could not believe it.'

Skinny ran one hand through his hair, front to back, then went on quickly.

'Lips said he didn't have the money right then but that he had more than that out. Much more. He said he had made a connection for two hundred thousand sets of Tees-and-Blues. Two hundred thousand, Curbel. He even had the address in his pocket. Skinny brought him to his car and put him in the trunk.'

Skinny had been looking past me as he spoke, very rapidly, almost to himself. His nostrils were flared, and his eyes were flicking back and forth, glistening.

Glistening with what? I wondered.

I asked, 'What's a Tee-and-Blue?'

He snorted, 'Tees-and-Blues, man,' and shot me an impatient glance. 'Two pills. One's an antihistamine, diethyl-methyl-something, like you use to keep your nose from running when you have a cold; the other's a mild analgesic, a painkiller not much stronger than aspirin. But burn 'em down together and hit 'em up, and they're righteous, like heroin but more jagged.'

'What are you talking about?' I asked, leaning back against a post and crossing my arms on my chest.

Skinny looked dumbfoundedly at me, then began his explanation again, speaking very slowly now and very deliberately, as if to a child.

'You take the two pills, melt them down together, inject them. If you do the antihistamine by itself, all you get is thirsty; the painkiller by itself won't cure a good headache. But in combination they have an effect like heroin but not so smooth. The advantage is, they're cheap, and there aren't too many rich junkies, right? I mean, you hear about old ladies ordering up from their butlers, but most junkies are shoplifting their way through their habits. Tees-and-Blues get them by for about half the price—they were big a few years ago, then they just sort of went away.'

I rubbed my forehead, acting more

confused than I was, using the hand to cover my eyes as I glanced at Skinny's arms, looking for needle marks.

He saw what I was doing and stuck his tongue out at me, curling it back toward his nose.

'I shoot up under my tongue. There and between my toes. You want Skinny to pull off his boot?'

There was a hard challenge in his voice, but he tossed his head and his tone changed.

'Anyway, we're not talking drugs here, we're talking money. At your local pharmacy by prescription the pills cost about eight cents each; but on the street, together, the set is selling for a nickel—a nickel is five dollars.'

'I know what a nickel is,' I said.

'Skinny never knows what you know, Curbel.' He worked a finger around his gums, turned his head to spit out a seed, looked back at me. 'How did you ever get through a year in jail?'

I rubbed my lower lip thoughtfully, pressing it against my teeth, and in that moment I caught an image of my father at his desk, his thinning gray hair ruffled back, glasses low on his nose, one finger pressed against his lower lip as he concentrated, sitting in the strange way he sat when he read his correspondence, poised, legs bent under him as if he were ready to spring at the letter he held; and I wondered how he had gotten so turned around, caught up in such meanness.

I asked Skinny, 'What was the address Lips had in his pocket?'

'Oh, yeah,' Skinny said again, shrugging indifferently but smirking before he went on. 'Skinny checks out the address and gets to other lines besides. It all comes up the same: a deposit has been made. There's big money in it. Two hundred thousand sets of Tees-and-Blues are as good as in the works—the profit for somebody will be close to three quarters of a million dollars.'

Three quarters of a million dollars, I thought.

'Meantime Skinny's got Lips in the trunk, and he's leaving the car running, making sure Lips gets a good dose of fumes. When the deal checks out, Skinny backs up on the levee and tells Lips to run it down to him, from the beginning, or he'll let the car roll into the river, ass end first. Lips gulps down some air and tells Skinny the rape charge is bogus. Skinny makes some more calls and starts to believe him because, guess what? The girl who charged him is from Central America. And before you get all excited about an ethnic slur, guess what else? The address she gave for the arrest report is the agency motel out on Airline Highway—too cozy to be coincidence, right? She's working for your family, Curbel.'

Skinny paused for a beat, whether to see if I would question him or to gloat, it was hard to tell which; I looked down and studied my shoes, pulling the toes back toward myself, watching the soft leather flex.

'It's all around you, man,' he added, sneering, 'Like a bad smell.'

I looked up and saw Skinny watching me, grinning rudely.

I did not say anything but stood up straight and pushed myself away from the post, just looking at him, not putting a lot into it but looking steadily, feeling my lips purse and the muscles tense in my jaw, my weight shifting, finding a balance on the balls of my feet; and I stood like that, poised but just looking at him until he backed off, raising and dropping both shoulders at once, flapping his arms in his comical way. He looked at his car, checking it, then he turned back, scratching the stubble on his cheeks with his fingertips, his restless eyes again flicking back and forth, but thoughtful now and seemingly vacant until they locked on me defiantly.

'Skinny *was* an addict,' he said, his tone harsh. 'He did shoot up under his tongue, Curbel. And under his balls. In his eyes.' He used one finger to pull down on his cheek until his lower eyelid stretched grotesquely. 'Anywhere you couldn't see it. Name a spot, Skinny's had a needle there.' He jerked his hand away from his face. 'Skinny's got six years and five months clean-time behind him. You can't understand that unless you've been there, but that makes Skinny one in a thousand, maybe one in ten thousand. So big fucking deal to you, right?'

I tried to hold his hot gaze but I felt myself sag, and my eyes slipped away.

'Six and a half years Skinny's hated that shit because he loves it so much. He traded his wife for it, and he went to jail for it—he got out of jail for it, just like you, by going undercover, snuggling up to the people who meant the most to him so that he could bust their ass. And he hasn't touched it. Not fucking once, got it?' He jabbed his finger at the air. 'Not fucking once.'

He waved his arm in his loose-jointed way, dismissing his own vehemence.

'So this is important to him.' He crossed his arms on his chest, tightly, as if trying to hold them still. 'So Skinny insulted your family when maybe he shouldn't have.' He looked directly at me. 'So he's sorry.'

I saw what he was doing—how he was attempting to offset rudeness with revelation—but there was something about his attempt to be persuasive that was itself unpersuasive, his tone, perhaps, the misplaced anger. His admission made me doubt he had ever been an addict in a more convincing way than if he had denied it, and I wondered whether or not I should be relieved, pleased, at least, that he did not need the drugs for his own personal use.

After a moment I nodded, that barely perceptible movement of my head that shows me my own uncertainty.

Skinny smiled shallowly, uneasily, and ran one hand over his face.

'The way Skinny figures it is this,' he began again, not so animated now, his tone curt. 'Lips was strapped coming up with the ten percent money for the bondsman, but he didn't want to stay in jail—that's easy to understand, right? He has connections but no cash, so he gets on the phone offering deals, trying to trade his connections for cash up front. It's a risk for him but he's a three-time loser, and he's looking at ninety-nine years, anyway. It's all he's got. DeLloyd hears about it—or maybe DeLloyd put him in the trick in the first place to get to his connections—and springs him so he can make the deal. So far, so good. Total risk: Fifteen thousand dollars and a false police report. But Lips comes through, and there has to be a deposit. Still no problem, right? There's a thirty-day float just looking for an investment. The deposit is made from the float, but the man on the other end is slow to deliver. The clock is ticking and thirty days later, it is getting very tense. And that's where it is right now. The Tees are already in—that's the address Lips had in his pocket, the storehouse for the two hundred thousand Tees—and the Blues are on the way.'

Skinny reached into his pocket and for a moment I thought he was reaching again for his silver revolver; but he came out instead with a piece of chewing gum.

I asked as he unwrapped it, 'How did you find out about the float?'

He looked at me curiously, folded the gum and put it into his mouth, chewed once.

'The girl told me, Curbel.' He chewed again, twice. 'How do you think?'

There was a knocking sound from his car, a muffled thumping. Skinny turned, opened the trunk, bent from the waist to listen. After a moment he nodded and reached into the trunk, then leaned back and slammed it. When he looked back at me he was smiling, genuinely amused.

'Lips has to go pee-pee,' he said, dropping a handful of corn husks into the gutter, brushing his palms one past the other. 'And he doesn't want to go in his pants.'

He ran his tongue over his lips, and the momentary amusement left his face. His voice became curt again, teacherlike.

'Three things make a deal, Curbel: people, drugs, and money. Skinny's on top of the first two. He'd like you to check out the third.'

I looked at him questioningly, wondering both what he meant and why he had made it a request.

'He wants you to see the girl,' he explained. 'Tonight, if you can. See if you can get a look at the books.'

He took out his keys and shook them.

'You find out about the money, you'll find out about your father—that Skinny guarantees.' He smiled brightly and put both his hands flat against his chest, fingers spread and squeezing obscenely. 'Anything else you get a look at is *your* business.'

He dropped his hands, turned away, picked up two more ears of corn, and waved them at the heavyset man at the table down the walk.

'Hey, son of a bitch,' he called. 'You better get down here. Skinny's taking your corn.'

He smiled at me again, moved behind his car, turned sideways, and slipped down the narrow space between the car and the truck close behind him.

'Think about it, Curbel,' he said loudly, over the roof of the car, over the sound of the rain drumming on the hood. 'You find out about the money, you may find out who sent you to jail.' He opened the car door, banging it against the side of the truck. 'And Tony,' he added condescendingly, twisting around, angling back as he squeezed through the door opening, 'give the fat man a dollar.'

CHAPTER EIGHT

Just after Skinny left the rain stopped as quickly as it had begun, and I used the first pay phone I found to call Stacey Veldran, dialing the number DeLloyd had written for me. Stacey lived out of the French Quarter, in the Garden District, and after I had spoken with her I decided to walk the thirty-odd blocks to her house, both pleased by the prospect of exercise—of being able to walk more than a few feet without encountering a steel wall—and enjoying the thick smells that seemed to hang in the humid air, so different from the jail's pervasive odor of close men and disinfectant.

As I walked the length of the French Quarter I smelled freshly ground coffee and chicory, garbage and barrooms, rancid oyster shells that had been tossed out on the sidewalk, back in the burlap sacks in which they had come, creamy white insides turned out, oysterless, shucked and slurped. I passed an open door and was hit by a blast of air-conditioned air, sanitized and odorless, and that light, false freshness seemed to last through downtown; the Garden District smelled of plants and decaying leaves.

The power lines hummed overhead, crackling when drops collected in the trees and fell, spattering against the high-voltage wires; and the regularly spaced streetlights hummed at a different pitch, lower and steadier, and made pockets of purple light between which there were dark shadows. Because the sidewalk was broken and uneven, whole sections of it lifted by the roots of huge trees that snaked as far as the curb, I walked in the street, stepping around puddles and potholes, listening to my wet shoes slapping against the pavement, speaking calmly to dogs that barked as they charged up behind iron fences. In one particularly long block I stopped to admire a carefully tended old house with fresh paint, a neat yard, warm yellow lights behind double-hung windows and thin gauzelike curtains; and just for a moment I envied the occupants the security of their lives. I wondered how they had managed it, the calmness and peace.

A patrol car came up behind me and fixed me in its harsh white spotlight before it moved past me slowly, the patrolman waving in a friendly way, acknowledging, I supposed, my coat and tie, my age, my light skin.

It could be worse, I thought, walking away before the patrol car made the block.

Stacey Veldran lived in a raised cottage that was set well back from the street, behind the high hedges, and set up on brick footings that raised its floor level four feet. The steps and porch were painted gray; the house was painted white. Over the windows were dark green louvered shutters. The front door was half cut glass with patterns that refracted the light and made it sparkle as I moved toward it, going up the walk, up the stairs, across the pleasant front porch.

When I rang the bell I heard her steps, high heels on bare wood, before I saw her—or the dark shape of her—through the sparkling glass. She opened the door and stood to one side without greeting me, her dark eyes calm and level, one eyebrow arched higher than the other. After a moment she said, 'I put on coffee,' and simply walked away from the open door, leaving me to come inside and close it, which I did.

Inside, the air was warm and the smell of her perfume lingered, rich and sweet. I followed the sound of her steps through the house, noting first the high ceilings and then her furniture, which on first impression seemed eclectic and rather too feminine, too colorful, without sharp corners, somehow more festive than I would have expected; then the bare white walls, completely unadorned, without pictures or paintings or prints.

The kitchen was brightly lit, warm, and functional. Copper-bottomed pots, long spoons, and strainers hung from a rack on the wall. The floor was made from big squares of tile. The counters were made of white maple. Without seeming to notice my presence

Stacey Veldran poured milk into a small pitcher, coffee into two cups, slid a bowl of sugar within easy reach; then she picked up a cup for herself and stepped back, leaning against the sink, stirring her black coffee slowly, thoughtfully, absorbed in the way it swirled about.

I stepped forward and picked up the other cup, added sugar, said 'Thanks.'

The coffee was fresh, very rich and smooth, very different from the oily, bitter coffee to which I had grown accustomed.

I watched her remove the small spoon from her cup, raise it upside down in her right hand, slowly, looking at it before her lips parted to receive it, reflexly closing over it as she pulled it back out, the shape of the spoon's shallow bowl momentarily forming the shape of her full lips as the shiny silver emerged, glistening.

She put the spoon down on the counter, wrapped her arm around her waist, looked at me, and asked, 'What can I do for you, Mr. Curbel?' pronouncing my name with the vowels very hard, almost accusingly, as if the name alone were some grave fault. It was a tone I had heard before, the first time in Mochita, that summer I had wandered the Curbelo plantation. And it surprised me.

'I'd like to see your books,' I said, coming directly to the point.

She raised on eyebrow in mild surprise.

‘Original entries will do,’ I added. ‘Or ledger entries—however you keep track of the collections.’

She put her cup down on the counter, next to the spoon, and for a long moment she stared at it blankly; then her eyes came back to me.

‘Of course,’ she said quietly, but with an edge.

I remembered that, too, that sullen acquiescence.

‘Let me get my cigarettes,’ she said. ‘Why don’t you wait in the den?’ and with that she left the kitchen abruptly, her heels clicking sharply against the tile.

I refilled my cup from the pot on the stove before I left the kitchen, too.

The den was across from the kitchen and I went in and waited there, standing up, idly looking toward the books on the shelves but not taking in the titles because I was remembering Stacey’s tone too clearly, recalling the first time I had heard it: then it had come from a Honduran field boss who had seen me watching his crew at work, and he had frightened me when he had come up to me, machete in hand, his lean body all cords and wiry muscles, gold teeth flashing when he said, ‘So you’re the new Curbelo, eh, who gets the run of the place?’ smiling when he said it but putting such a hard edge on the words I had looked past him, figuring the distance to my grandmother's house—and safety. But the house had been too far away, across a thousand acres of cane, so I had dug down deep within myself and replied harshly, with a defiance equal to my fear, '*Yo soy Curbelo*,' and he had looked down at his machete—just as Stacey had looked down a few moments before—and said, '*Por supuesto*' (Of course), quietly, but with that same edge.

I turned away from the bookshelves, looked out at the yard, looked at the door in time to see Stacey come in carrying two carousel slide trays in one hand and a pack of cigarettes in the other. She put both on the table behind her couch, then left again, returning shortly thereafter with her cup of coffee and a heavy, clear glass ashtray.

She lit a cigarette, took a deep pull on it, put it in the ashtray.

'How far back would you like to go?' she asked, exhaling smoke after the question, lifting a projector from beside the table up onto it.

'Six months should do it,' I replied, and I watched as she examined the slide trays, chose one, put it on the projector.

'Ellis told me to keep a copy of the accountings I gave him,' she explained, standing up straight and retrieving her cigarette from the ashtray, flicking the ash from the end of it before she glanced at me. 'He said the easiest way would be to photograph my book. He showed me how—he knows a lot about cameras.'

'I know,' I said.

When she turned on the projector its harsh white light glared against the wall, and she left it shining like that, glaring, as she moved to a switch on the wall. Before she flipped the switch—turning off the other lights in the room—I saw her give me the same look she had given me that morning: an openly assessing look, full of resentment, but with something else in it, too, something much harder, contempt, perhaps, or scorn.

She advanced the projector, and the image of an unlined notebook appeared. The notebook was lying flat, open; there were figures in the center of the page and notations around the margins. I stepped close to the image and tried to read it, but while the figures were clear enough—the debits were on the left, credits on the right—the writing in the margins was tiny and angular, impossible to read.

'This is illegible,' I said, shaking my head.

'Ellis can read it,' she replied flatly.

She walked around the couch and stood in the bright light, in front of me, near enough to touch, the figures and writing now projected on her too, lost in her gray skirt but clear on her white blouse.

'It's simple enough,' she said.

When she looked at me through that harsh

glare her eyes were as shiny as glass; near her pupils were brilliant hard pinpoints of light.

'The numbers on the right show what we actually collected. On the left are the amounts deferred'—she pointed to the marginal notations—'and the reasons why we deferred them.'

I looked again at the writing, studying it. After a moment I said, 'I can't read it,' and shook my head again.

I turned back to her and saw that she was watching me, her dark eyes aware and assessing, playing over me coolly but impatiently, irritably.

I flicked my eyes away, to the image on the wall, and asked, 'After you receive a payment, how long is it before you post the entry?'

'Why don't you ask your uncle?' she replied wearily, snidely, the contempt I had seen before now fully revealed in her tone.

'Because I asked *you*,' I snapped, turning a hard, challenging glance on her, tired of her barely concealed hostility, her needless antagonism.

'The entries are made after every transaction,' she said.

I nodded once curtly.

'That's fine,' I replied, then ordered, 'Let's see the next slide.'

She cocked her head to one side, looking past me now, through me, unable or unwilling to hold my hard gaze.

'As you wish,' she said, turning away to change the slide but glancing back at me as she did so, out of the corners of her eyes.

I recognized that furtive glance, too.

The next slide appeared.

I took a final sip from my coffee and put the empty cup on one of the shelves behind me.

She looked at the cup, looked down, moved docilely to pick it up.

I saw what she was doing and said, 'Stop it,' harshly.

She knew exactly what I meant.

One hand went to the collar of her blouse and adjusted it nervously, pulling it close. She started to turn away, but I put my hand on her elbow and held it, not tightly but firmly, looking at her, waiting for her to look back at me.

I wanted to say 'Your problems are not my fault,' but she said, 'I'm sorry,' first, quietly, looking down.

There was a surreal, otherworldly quality to the way she appeared at that moment—her face divided vertically, half in shadow, the other half glowing, bright white against the darkness behind her; each hair on her head shining brilliantly, individually; the glass-hard light in one eye—and for a moment I wondered if I was not projecting my feelings onto her, giving each small sign more than its due, enhancing her, but when she dropped her glance like that, contritely, artfully, I could have laughed out loud because there was so much of Ellis in that sudden change, the way she shifted moods like gears, working through the contempt and sullenness I had seen, then refuting them quickly, just as Ellis worked through his stories, focusing attention one way, then shifting that focus unexpectedly, advantagously. So I released her arm and just stood there, waiting to see what would follow, somehow not surprised when she looked up expectantly, provocatively, lips parted; but I felt a chill nonetheless, a bristling coldness on the nape of my neck when her unambiguous glance played over me.

One hand was still at her collar. I took it and pulled it down, to her side. Just then it did not matter to me what she was up to or why she might need advantage over me: I had been a year in jail, and I had need of her, too—her reasons could be her own. My eyes took in the fullness of her hips, her narrow waist, the swell of her breasts.

Her face now was smooth, relaxed, very confident. She looked down, then up, her glance lingering, waiting.

Slowly I reached through the space of harsh light between us and pulled her blouse aside, exposing one breast, openly looking at it, seeing its fullness, the pale pink nipple; I took it in my hand and cupped it, lifting it slightly, shifting my gaze as I did so, seeing the long curve of her throat, her strong, firm jaw, the light behind the light in her eyes, distant and mocking.

I rolled her nipple between thumb and first finger, pinching it, watching her reaction, pinching harder until her eyes half-closed and the light glinted behind her lashes, gleaming malevolently, all pretense gone.

I released her nipple and stepped to one side, looking back at the light, moving my hand down, between her breasts, down over the cool soft skin on her belly, seeing the downlike hair glowing, golden along the dark round shapes of her; with my other hand I found the clasp on her skirt and the zipper. Her skirt loosened and fell as my hand continued down, tracing its own course. I pulled her blouse up and back, away, off. Between her legs she was very warm, deep warm, and moist; the skin was thin and exquisitely soft.

The projector's fan motor hummed, the only sound.

Just for a moment I thought of my wife, without anger about her death, remembering how we both had given, each to the other, and I stood very still, feeling her loss, wanting her and not this taking, this calculated exchange.

Stacey ran her fingers down my chest, bent

her head to my belly; her tongue was warm where she licked, then abruptly each spot was cold as she moved on, pulling me down smoothly, deftly, and I was on her full-length, in her deeply, driving myself at her over and over, hearing the violent slapping sound, flesh against flesh.

She watched me, a violet color deep in her eyes, and I watched her watching me, feeling mechanical and tireless, wanting to do more than to penetrate her but to make her feel, more than feel, to feel *me*. She seemed to sense that and very suddenly she turned, rolling under me to face away. She pushed up to all fours, crouched like a wrestler, leaning back. I ran my hands along her sides, reaching under her to feel her breasts, hanging, then down her ribs to the flare of her hips, parting them roughly.

She tensed, quivering slightly.

I pulled my lip between my teeth.

The quiet was unsettling, very different from the jail's constant noise of radios tuned to different stations, steel doors slamming, the hard echoes of unending talk.

Don't think, I thought, but as I rose up over her, my hands tightening, thumbs and fingertips pressed deep into her flesh, I heard the screams I had heard in my bunk at night, the terrified, panic-filled sounds that had shot through the constant noise; and I thought of Randy, of the price he would pay for the smeared tattoo on his hand—the deal I had struck for him. I pictured the glassy-eyed biker, brown tobacco spittle drooling down his chin, long greasy hair falling over his face in clumps as he crouched as I was crouched, thumbs and fingertips pressed deeply into flesh, parting it, rising up and moving his cold flaccid gut forward, and down. In my chest I felt the hollow feeling I had felt as I had lain in my bunk, powerless, hearing those screams, then listening involuntarily, helplessly, for the baleful, wounded-animal whimpering that would follow; and I felt the same sag, the empty anger, sadness, and disgust I had felt when later those low whining moans had come and were answered with hoots of derisive laughter.

As if on their own my hands loosened and fell away from Stacey's hips. Slowly I sat back on my heels, then I pushed back farther and sat up on the couch, not wanting to look at her, looking up instead, at the bright numbers projected on the wall. I brought my hand up and rubbed my knuckles against my cheek, listening to the dull scraping sound my whiskers made.

At the edge of my vision I saw Stacey stand up, collect her clothes, move behind me. Before she left the room she put her hand over my shoulder, indecisively, as if she were about to touch me, then she pulled it away. I heard her bare feet on the bare wood floor, then I heard a door close down the hall. Behind me the projector's fan motor hummed, a steady insistent drone.

After a while I stood up, adjusted my clothes, went into the kitchen to get another cup of coffee. In the kitchen window I saw my reflection, and I tried to examine my eyes as I smoothed down my shirt and hitched up my pants; but about my face the reflection was dark and shadowy, ghostlike, too dim to see clearly. I went back out into the corridor and looked down toward the closed door to Stacey's room, then returned to the den.

The projector was still running, and before I turned it off idly I advanced through the slides of her account book, looking at the first few pages carefully but seeing very quickly that all the pages were as indecipherable as the two I had already seen. So I held the button down and allowed the projector to set its own speed, not really looking at the slides that flashed but waiting for the carousel to come full circle, back to the beginning of the tray; but when a flash of color appeared, strikingly warm and bright after the harsh black and white that had preceded it, I stopped, only after a few moments realizing that those bright colors formed a picture of my father's house, the house where I had been raised. Seeing it like that, very suddenly just there in a resplendent, high-intensity image, for a moment I seemed able to see the house, of itself, without the emotional content my memories of it brought.

Despite its steeply pitched roof the house was very horizontal, lower and longer than I remembered it. The small windows were very square and unadorned, without shutters or shades. The yard was cut short and edged carefully, precisely contained within its allotted space, not a blade of grass out of place. It struck me that the house was very austere, functional in an overdisciplined, rigid way that somehow reminded me of a low ship on calm water, battened down for rough going.

I advanced the projector curiously.

The next picture showed my father at the door to his house, caught, surprised in a very bright flash. His gray hair was neatly combed, but his jaw was slack and his eyes had the wet-glassy look they get when he has been drinking. He wore the red-and-white-checked cowboy shirt he saves for special occasions and the belt buckle I had given him as a none-too-subtle joke to go along with it—the flash had reflected on the shiny two-inch-high brass letters that spelled out his name, Carl, and on the huge silver sheriff's star on which they were mounted. Behind him an afternoon party was in progress; people I did not recognize were clustered in small groups, cocktails in hand, smiling and talking politely. Although I had never seen it before, that picture seemed as familiar to me as the house itself and the memories it contained, each one distinct, my father at the center, the steady anchor around which I swung. Yet even as I examined that picture and acknowledged the power of my memories—the sway my father held over me—I realized there was some distance between what I was and what I had been, a thought that gave me reassurance because it was important to me not to confuse the two: particularly at that moment, I did not feel prepared to dwell in that past.

The phone rang, and it startled me; I was startled again when Stacey answered it. She was behind me, near the door, dressed now in a thigh-length white terry cloth bathrobe, a pillow and blanket held under one arm.

She listened, spoke softly into the phone, nodded once.

I glanced at her then away, feeling awkward, noting with some regret the smooth firmness of her legs and the enticing space between them as she stood, feet apart, hip cocked to one side, leaning down so that the hem of her bathrobe moved up.

After a brief conversation she hung up the phone, turned on the lights, moved past me, and dropped the blanket and pillow on the couch.

'That was Ellis,' she said, turning to face me, her expression drawn but more forgiving than I might have expected. 'He called earlier, too. DeLloyd told him about the two men at your apartment.' She waved one hand, indicating the blanket and pillow she had dropped on the couch. 'He wants you to stay here.'

I stood quietly because I did not know what to say to her.

Her right hand moved to her left arm and rubbed it, elbow to shoulder, then her glance moved to the picture of my father on the wall, dimmer now with the room lights on but still very clear.

'I took that last month. Do you want to see the rest?'

I shook my head, no—I had seen enough for one evening.

She acknowledged my refusal with a resigned frown, a slight turning down at the corners of her lips; she reached forward as if to snap off the projector but advanced it instead.

A picture of my father and Ellis appeared. They were standing side by side in my father's living room, Ellis on the left, towering over his brother, and while they were both smiling dutifully for the camera, their unease was apparent in the way they stood: Ellis, his weight on his good leg, his bad leg stuck out in front of him, arms crossed forbiddingly on his chest; my father, drink in hand but more sober looking now, left arm held stiffly at his side, chin ducked down impatiently.

They do not look like brothers, I thought, allowing my eyes to move back and forth, comparing their features. *They do not even look like friends.*

'They don't get together very often,' Stacey said with finality, and a bit too pensively, I thought, wistfully but in a contrived sort of way; she turned off the projector, dismissing them both.

I watched the colors fade quickly, within the space of a second, just then wondering how pictures of my father's party happened to be in with the pictures of her account book.

'What else did Ellis want?' I asked, looking at her again, nodding toward the phone.

'Nothing, really,' she replied, distracted. She unplugged the projector and put it back in its place on the floor. 'There's a bathroom down the hall,' she said.

She put her hands in the pockets of her robe.

'He's having trouble getting to sleep,' she added. Her eyes slipped off me and looked at a point somewhere on the floor. 'Last night he dreamed that your father was dead.'

I felt a light chill run up my spine and a flush come into my cheeks. I seemed to see her very clearly just then—her eyes were cast down, concealed by her lashes, and her lips were pressed together tightly, thoughtfully—

and I started to say something but I did not because behind her on the shelf, as if by magic, three big books jumped straight up. Simultaneously I felt a stinging on my neck and ear; I heard a huge roar.

Glass broke against the floor.

For a long moment I just stood there, not comprehending what had happened, seeing Stacey's eyes grow huge in the soft light, then something in me clicked and I moved very quickly, instinctively grabbing her and dropping to the floor, catching an image of Ellis's old Enfield rifle as a second high-velocity shot ripped through the room.

More glass sprayed. A lamp fell.

I curled up, holding Stacey tightly, forcing her into a ball, waiting for the next shot, knowing at some place deep within myself the rhythm of rapid fire, the bolt yanked open, hull extracted ringing, the bolt slammed home again as the cheek sought a place on the stock and the barrel dropped into line.

We lay very still, breathing shallowly, my elbow crushed beneath Stacey's side.

I could feel my heart's wild thumping.

No third shot came.

I pressed my eyes closed, opened them.

Very slowly, tentatively, I relaxed my hold.

No third shot came. I rolled away from her and heard in the distance the high-low wail of a police siren, getting closer.

I could still feel my heart thumping.

* * *

We walked behind the policeman as he went from the den to the living room to the front porch, stopping at each wall along the way to shine his long black flashlight at the holes the bullets had made, inspecting them. He was a big man, shapelessly broad in the hips and shoulders, thick through the middle, and his presence was reassuring.

'It looks like this one went all the way through,' he said matter-of-factly, turning to Stacey and me, resting his hand on the butt of his revolver.

'All the way *through*?' Stacey asked incredulously. 'Through my *house*?'

He smiled easily.

'It won't be hard to fix,' he said.

There was a knocking on the living room wall, and the policeman reached up, over his head, to grab the long, thin rod his partner had pushed through the hole. He pulled the rod through, then pulled gently at the bright red knitting yarn that was tied to the end of it. As his arm moved up and down, pulling the yarn until it was taut, his badge flashed where it was pinned to his chest, the porch lights reflecting on the shiny silver surface of the odd design, a sweeping Turkish crescent over a five-pointed star.

'Let's see how we did,' he said finally, and

moved past us, into the house.

We walked behind him again, the length of the house, all three of us looking at the bright red yarn that traced the slightly divergent paths the bullets had taken. One bullet had struck the fireplace in the living room and exploded a hole in the brick the size of my fist; the other—the one that had gone right through—had traveled a foot lower and to the left.

In the den I looked down the yarn, through the broken window, and saw quite clearly where the lines would intersect: there was an opening in the thick hedges, a low chainlink gate, and behind the gate was the street.

The policeman said, 'Just stand where you were when you heard the first shot.'

Stacey and I moved obediently to where we had been; our eyes locked briefly, then we both looked away. To my right, at arm's length, chest high, the red yarn stretched, moving upward at a slight angle.

The policeman took a small, collapsible camera from his hip pocket and unfolded it; he looked through it, checked the settings, looked at me curiously.

'Weren't you out earlier?' he asked.

'Yes,' I replied, remembering the police car that had passed me on my walk to Stacey's house, its bright spotlight, the policeman waving in a friendly way.

'I thought so,' he said, and snapped the

picture.

The camera made a humming sound and spat out a square of white paper. Without looking at it the policeman took it and handed it to me, said, 'Hold this for me—it'll dry in a minute,' and moved out into the hallway to take more pictures.

I held the damp paper carefully, allowing it to lie flat on my outstretched palm. Stacey stood beside me, and together we watched the image develop, the colors seeming to grow. In the picture the yarn showed up exceptionally well, two angry red lines just behind us.

* * *

Stacey made the policemen wait, refusing to let them leave until she dressed and packed a small overnight bag. She left the lights in her house turned on, and as we drove away, I saw them glowing behind the double-hung windows and the thin gauzelike curtains, warmly, not different at all from the house I had stopped to admire.

Dressed in tan linen slacks and a very white and crisp cotton blouse, Stacey appeared composed, fresh, more distracted than disturbed—although she was very quiet, turned into herself, sedate in too thoughtful a way, the silence between us was easy. I asked her where we were going; she replied that she did not know. As she drove, one at a time, as if testing them, she bent the nails on her fingers against the sides of her thumbs.

Out near the airport we found a high-rise motel and checked in, paying cash so that we could use a false name, tacitly agreeing to share a room, parking way out in back, near a Dumpster. When we were in the elevator, she noticed the small cuts on my neck; in the room, perfunctorily she removed what glass she could find and swabbed them. In the distance we could see the airport and the beacon that turned on top of the tower. The pale gray light seemed to move very slowly until it flashed by.

Separately we undressed and got into bed. The sheets were cool and crisp; the bed was huge and firm, very different from the bunk I was used to. In the darkness I could feel the tension between us. I knew that she was as awake as I was, but we lay unmoving, neither speaking nor touching. After a while I dozed and in my sleep started to roll away, and only then did I feel her hold to me tightly, almost fearfully, as if she were seeing something there in the darkness, as if at some end I could not understand.

CHAPTER NINE

In the morning, Stacey slept as I ordered from room service, shaved with a razor I found in her bag, took a long shower. Because I had left my briefcase—and the razor and fresh shirt I had packed in it—with the bartender in the bar I had visited, I would have to wear the same shirt I had worn the day before; and that bothered me. I smiled at myself in the mirror, only partly amused by how quickly my priorities changed.

I did not know what I should do first, whether I should see Ellis and try to find out what he knew about the float or see Skinny and try to convince him to abandon his plans for the deal: I did not know which was wiser, to try to overtake events or to become a part of them, trying to hasten their end. I was tempted to confide in Stacey and to ask her advice, but I did not know that I could trust her, whether or not she was using me for some purpose I could not then see—or what she might want in return. I remembered the way she had held me the night before, clutching to me, and I wondered how much she knew.

There was a knock at the door, and as I crossed the room to answer it, I saw Stacey sit up in bed and adjust the sheet, pulling it around herself and holding it in place with one arm. I signed for the coffee and toast, turned back to her, put the tray on the low dresser. I remembered that she drank coffee black, poured her a cup, took it, and handed it to her.

She sipped it, made a face at its taste, put it on the bedside table.

I poured myself a cup, added milk and sugar, and turned back to her. Stacey seemed unfocused—sleepy or distracted—so I crossed my arms on my chest and shifted my glance away from her, sipping my coffee, observing the airport in the distance and a large airplane rising at a steep angle away from it.

I looked back when she said, 'I have to stop by the agency,' flatly, matter-of-factly. 'After that,' she added, 'I have to go out to New Orleans East.'

There was no warmth in her voice, nothing to indicate the night we had shared. She reached back to the bedside table, moved the coffee aside, and picked up her cigarettes and lighter.

'Is that very smart?' I asked, allowing it to go her way, questioning only the wisdom of being seen at the agency and not her coolness toward me. 'What about Señor Esperoza?'

'What about him?' she said tiredly, and put a cigarette in her mouth. She lit and blew the smoke through her nose. 'We don't know that it *was* Esperoza.'

My eyes caught hers.

'It may have been DeLloyd,' she added.

That surprised me. I took a sip of coffee as I considered the possibility, recalling DeLloyd's extraordinarily rapid movements, how his fist had caught the solid man first on the cheek, then on the temple, with such force the man had slammed against the bathroom wall and bounced, knees buckling; then picturing him behind the low gate in the darkness, standing very still, a rifle held to his shoulder, his brown-black eyes half-closed as he sighted down the barrel into the den where Stacey and I were standing—but I could not make that image of him fit.

DeLloyd would use his hands, I thought.

When Stacey again reached for her coffee, I asked, 'Would you like some sugar in that?' and she nodded that she would. She picked up the cup and held it out to me.

I stepped over to the bed, took the cup, stepped back to the dresser. I poured sugar into the coffee, stirred it, asked, 'What's in New Orleans East?'

Stacey was slow to reply, and as I started back to her, looking at the coffee, not looking where I was going, I stubbed my toe against the foot of the bed. When I jerked back, hot coffee spilled over my hand. I swore and with effort held my hand very still, long enough not to spill more.

Stacey was not amused by my clumsiness.

Irritably she flicked an ash at the ashtray, looked out the window.

The coffee had sloshed more than spilled. I pulled out the corner of the sheet to wipe my hand. The sheet billowed, and beneath it I caught a glimpse of her bare legs; I wiped my hand, then the cup, and set the cup beside her on the table. Stacey just looked at it, seeming to look right through it, at some point in the distance.

After a while, she said, 'You know, Tony,' her eyes moving from the cup to the dresser to me, 'if I had just spent a year in jail, I think I'd want to find out who had put me there. I think I'd want to find out what had happened.'

I cocked my head to one side, my eyes narrowing, not really understanding what she was getting at but resenting her tone, her cool condescension.

'I think I'd try to see the connections—'

'Get to the point, Stacey,' I said softly, but with an edge. She mashed out her cigarette.

'Ellis's truck stop is in New Orleans East.'

I looked at her quizzically. 'His truck stop?'

She fixed me in a hard, ill-tempered stare before she glanced away.

'The truck stop is where we cache the money we collect from the agency and our other little businesses. It's our bank.' She toyed with the ashtray, turning it. 'We have to keep it somewhere.' She tossed her head and looked back at me. 'Didn't you ever wonder where it all came from? All that money your *clients* had?'

I did not reply but looked at her steadily, my bland expression a mask.

Stacey collected the ashtray, her lighter, and cigarettes and set them beside her leg. She seemed to be organizing herself as she organized the small objects, mustering patience but doing it in an oddly coy, self-satisfied way.

'The agency is very profitable, Tony, and the other businesses have grown, too. DeLloyd and I collected the money from all of them—it's more than you might suspect—then Ellis recounted and verified it. But cash is a problem. You can't show too much of it without attracting attention; so once every two months your father picked it up and took it to Panama—once it was deposited there it was practically untraceable because the Panamanian bank secrecy laws are so strict. All your father had to do then was to get it back to this country, which he did by sending you *clients*. You exchanged it. He invested it.' Her voice took on a derisive edge. 'He said you were very clever about it.' She smiled artificially, on and off. 'The way you got around the currency laws was most amusing.'

'Where did it go then?' I asked, ignoring

her snide tone. 'After I had converted it back into dollars?'

'After that?' she replied coolly. 'After that we didn't have illegal cash, we had *foreign investors*—names to put on dummy accounts that your father controls. He uses the money as he sees fit.'

I allowed my eyes to wander to the window, giving myself a moment to think. What Stacey had said did not surprise me as much as the way she had said it. Again I did not understand her quick hostility, her needless antagonism. That snide tone was there too readily, its source in her running just beneath the surface; and I realized then that likely it had nothing to do with me, not me personally, but with what she thought I represented: the twenty thousand acres of Curbelo land, the Mochitan peasants kept in poverty to work it, the big white house she had seen from every window in her childhood.

I raised one hand, fingers extended, and rubbed my chin thoughtfully, rolling my head back, wondering if I should explain to her my own resentment, the price my name had extracted from me, too.

'You act as if you knew,' she said.

'I did,' I replied, not bothering to add that I had not known until my father had explained it to me, after I was arrested. Up until that time I had been content not to know, not to question even the most implausible *clients* because, it was obvious to me now, I did not want to acknowledge any threat to my pleasantly ordered world.

'I did,' I said again. 'I did know.'

Stacey's upraised face showed mild curiosity.

'Then perhaps there's something you can explain to me.'

I waved my hand noncommittally.

'Why did the money stop coming back up?'

'That,' I replied absently, 'I don't know—I didn't realize that it had.'

'It stopped just after you went to jail,' she said, then added softly, almost to herself, 'And it's not just sitting in Panama. They're spending it. All of it.'

'Spending it on what?' I asked, though it seemed to me not to matter.

She shook her head, her expression blank in an uncertain way.

I shrugged dismissively.

'Maybe they stopped exchanging the money because they couldn't replace me,' I suggested. 'Maybe they couldn't find anyone as clever.' I smiled, on and off. 'Or as amusing.'

Stacey's irritated glance flicked past me; in one motion she threw aside the sheet and stood up, pointedly ignoring me, moving past me to pick up her blouse and slacks from the chair where she had put them. She started toward the bathroom but stopped near the foot of the bed and turned back to me.

'You're not as clever as you think, Tony,' she said crossly, arranging her clothes on her arm. 'You haven't asked the big question, the one that ties it all together.'

'Oh?' I asked, raising my eyebrows, sorry that I had provoked her but maintaining a skeptical stance. 'What is that?'

She looked directly at me.

'You haven't asked which bank in Panama your father uses.'

It took a moment for me to understand why that was important, but when I did understand it I nearly said 'Damn' out loud. I felt foolish because I had played a game with her and I had *not* asked the right question.

'He uses the Banco de Santander,' Stacey pressed, a hard edge on her words. 'Señor Esperoza's bank.'

And Señor Esperoza wants to change the bank secrecy laws, I thought, remembering what Ellis had told me, understanding then why Ellis had not found it difficult to 'lose' Esperoza's sons: *a change in the laws would open the books*, I thought. *If Esperoza has his way, he will reveal the money, both how much there was and how we had laundered it. We would all go to jail.*

'I'm going to get dressed,' Stacey said coolly. 'After that I'll—'

'Wait.' I stopped her, giving myself time,

trying to put my thoughts in order, wondering what else I had missed, and wondering, too, why Ellis would claim not to have the two boys if he did. Inadvertently I put weight on the toe I had stubbed, felt a sharp pain, shifted my stance.

'After that,' Stacey repeated insistently, forcing me to look at her, 'I'll take you to see Ellis—I'll call when we're ready to leave.' She glanced at the phone speculatively, then returned her glance to me. 'Maybe Ellis will explain it to you,' she said.

She looked down and nervously picked a piece of lint from her blouse.

'There must be a good reason why he's willing to trade away your father.'

I ran my hand through my hair, front to back, and looked down, not wanting her to see my eyes.

He will do what he has to do, I thought, recalling my father's harsh words to me, feeling a chill run up my spine.

* * *

Ellis did not answer when Stacey tried to call him, and although I felt it was risky, rather than go to his shop to wait for him—which I felt was riskier still—I agreed to go with Stacey to the agency. She would use the phone there, she said, to try to call Ellis again. Before I closed the door to the room behind us, I looked to see what we had forgotten, noting the rumpled, unmade bed, the towels in a wet pile beside the sink, the coffee I had spilled on the dresser. In the elevator, Stacey looked at me coolly, then looked away, up over the double doors, and watched the floor numbers blink.

Before we got into the car, I said, 'This isn't very smart.'

She glanced at me over the roof of the car, and although she did not reply, I could see that she was frightened, too—it was in her still expression and in the nervous way she jangled her keys. As we drove away from the motel and turned onto Veterans Highway, we both looked around often, pretending to be casual as we studied each car that pulled up next to us or followed us too closely, looking for some sign but half-expecting bullets to smash through the car without warning, hearing the sound they would make, the terrifying high-velocity cracks we had heard the night before.

The small hairs on the back of my neck bristled.

Stacey lit a cigarette, then tamped it out, rattling the dashboard ashtray.

* * *

Veterans Highway was a treeless, eight-lane suburban strip lined with fast-food restaurants, automobile dealerships, and glass-fronted stores built side by side. Each one of the businesses visibly competed with its neighbors for attention, and huge flags waved, banners fluttered, bright signs and bright lights blinked. Even though it was early morning, traffic was very heavy and moved, it seemed to me, at reckless speed.

I looked out the passenger-side window of the car, reminding myself that my perception of speed was likely deceptive: the traffic to which I had grown accustomed moved at a short-distance, shuffling walk. I looked at my watch and remembered the lines that had formed for breakfast.

After a while I saw a store that seemed familiar, then a bright neon sign that I knew. Stacey braked sharply for a red light, and when the traffic in front of us cleared, I saw the agency two long blocks down. The one-story brick building seemed subdued, unimportant, nearly lost amid the roadside's flashy clutter.

'There wasn't much out here when the agency was built,' I said to Stacey, making conversation, relaxing a bit, recalling the way the highway had looked when my father had first driven me down it. 'All this was mostly uncleared.' I waved my hand in a sweeping gesture. 'Right over there'—I pointed to a used car lot—'was a riding stable.'

'I know,' she replied, not unkindly but

absently, looking into her purse, then looking back up, seeing that the light had changed, and accelerating quickly. 'Ellis used to take me there.'

'My father never did,' I said ruefully, smiling thinly.

As we turned into the driveway it seemed to me that the building resembled a doctor's clinic, low, turned inward, and undistinguished.

Stacey parked in back, and when she went inside I went in, too, noticing the peeling paint on the trim, the worn linoleum floor, the small cracks in the panels that covered the off-color fluorescent tubes.

'I won't be long,' she said, and went into an office.

I waited in the reception area, first sitting tentatively on one of the Fiberglas chairs, then standing up again, fidgeting but moving carefully, favoring my foot because the toe I had stubbed was still sore. Through the corner window I could see down the highway to the used car lot I had pointed out to Stacey, and as I looked at it, seeing the small, brightly colored flags that hung over it, idly I recalled the summer my father had brought me with him, every weekend, to inspect the work on the building that now seemed worn and rather tired. I recalled that, when newly poured, the pale gray slab on which the building rested had seemed like a low island in the deep black mud that surrounded it; I recalled the oppressive heat, the swarms of mosquitoes, my father in shirt-sleeves, blueprints in hand, walking around the slab as the building took shape, mumbling to himself, slapping the mosquitoes without seeming to notice them as he located the walls and rooms and paced them off and I waited sullenly near his car, deep in a teenager's moody ill humor, not wanting to be there and angry that he had forced me to come.

Ellis used to take me there, I thought, thinking then of Stacey and Ellis, picturing them in the dilapidated barn that I remembered from those trips.

Stacey had said it very simply, giving it no special significance, yet in a way it was a revelation. I could see them together, Ellis hobbling with difficulty through the mud, holding her hand as much for his balance as for hers as she pulled him along, timid but anxious. She would have had to request it carefully to get Ellis into a barnyard, and he would have agreed gruffly, begrudgingly, until the appointed day rolled around and his own good humor got the best of him, perhaps when he stepped in something unsavory and he rolled his eyes heavenward, smiling at himself, then to her. I pictured her in cowboy boots that were too big for her, wide-eyed around the tired, swaybacked horses; I heard her giggle at Ellis's expression. And as clear a picture as it formed—as easily as the image came to me, as if on its own, as if out of *my* past—I had to wonder why I had not met Stacey before, why her name had never been mentioned, not once, not even in passing. In people and places, in all but time, Stacey and I had overlapped so closely that for me not to know her, or at least to know *of* her, was clearly more than omission.

I ran one hand over my face, suddenly disturbed in an unsettling way. I could not think of Ellis without remembering very clearly how he had said, 'I gave your mother the polio that killed her,' flatly, kneading his leg; and I remembered how I had felt, the blood draining from my face, too stunned to object to his *story*, the deep coldness I had felt. The more I learned of my past, the more disturbing it became, and I did not want any more of it, not today.

Behind me I heard Stacey ask, 'Are you ready?'

I turned and walked toward her hesitantly, feeling cowardly in a peculiar sort of way, wanting to ask her about herself but knowing that I would not.

'Why are you limping?' she asked sharply, surprising me with a tone that was suddenly accusing, a mix of anger and fear.

'My toe,' I replied, stopping and pointing down, looking at her quizzically, seeing that her face was pale and drawn, almost fearful.

After a moment her expression relaxed somewhat and turned introspective. She looked past me, at the window.

'It must be the light . . .' she said softly, more to herself than to me, then her voice got stronger, and she added, 'The light was behind you.' She raised her purse waist high, clutching it with both hands in front of herself. 'For a moment you looked just like him,' she said. She smiled tightly. 'Like Ellis.'

I looked at her curiously, wondering what past *she* was confronting, what had brought the pale fear to her face.

Her eyes flicked past me. She looked down, opened her purse, and said, 'Ellis still doesn't answer at his shop,' as she plunged her hand wrist deep into the purse and busily rummaged through it. 'He may be at the truck stop—his darkroom is there.'

She took out her keys first, then a black leather wallet. She closed her purse and tucked it under her arm, holding it by pressing it between elbow and ribs.

'It's not much,' she said, and held the wallet out to me, looking at it.

I stepped forward and took it, surprised first by her offer, then by the wallet's solid weight. Curious to know what it was, I examined it closely and saw that it was not a wallet at all but an odd sort of case; I saw a clasp and twisted it, opening it, seeing as the two halves of the case came apart the small black pistol it contained. The pistol was short and ugly, worn on the barrel end and the butt.

'The safety is on the left,' she said.

I glanced up at her, then down again, looking at the pistol, studying it, reading the small square letters that were stamped into the slide.

'Whoever it was last night,' Stacey added too coolly, too matter-of-factly, shaking her keys, then forcing one finger through her key ring's tight wire loop, 'I don't think they were shooting at me.'

I thought about that for a moment, then closed the case, puzzled, irresolute, uncertain whether or not I should keep it.

What made you reach that conclusion just now, I wanted to ask, *just after you mistook me for my uncle?*

CHAPTER TEN

Between the motel on one side and the twenty-four-hour restaurant on the other, there was a huge parking lot, a flat expanse of black asphalt marked with broad white stripes; between the stripes, parked in rows, there were trucks, big eighteen-wheel open-road trucks, dozens of them, many with their engines running, making that throaty-clattery sound big diesels make at idle.

In the restaurant the main part of the dining room was marked off with a large sign that read ON-DUTY DRIVERS ONLY, and that part was very crowded. Though the faces of many of the drivers showed fatigue, a purposeful vitality was there, a vibrant hum of conversation. Country music played from a juke box. Reports of interstate highway conditions flashed on big color monitors that hung from the low, suspended ceiling. Waitresses hurried about, filling orders from the grill.

Stacey walked through the restaurant, then down a short corridor that had a small convenience store on one side and two-dollar showers on the other; and I followed just behind her. At the end of the corridor she pushed through an unmarked door into a small room that served as an office. Three desks were crowded together, almost touching, and on the far wall a large window looked out into the parking lot, out at the trucks.

Stacey moved behind the first desk, and as she examined the papers that were there, I went to the window and looked at the trucks in the parking lot, impressed with the truck stop and somehow understanding Ellis a little better for seeing it, understanding his cowboy boots and his stories, his disheveled two-room cottage; then I saw Ellis himself, out on the parking lot, hobbling into view around a truck, leaning heavily on his cane.

'He's here,' I said to Stacey.

A truck horn blared, and Ellis jumped awkwardly, startled, turning and glowering up at the long square hood of a truck that was as large as a chrome-trimmed shed. After a moment he smiled in recognition of the driver and waved his cane in a good-humored threat, banging it against the truck's massive, waist-high bumper as he hobbled around to the driver's side.

The driver leaned out of the window, spat a long brown jet of tobacco juice, and pushed his cowboy hat back on his head.

I felt Stacey come up beside me, but I kept my eyes on Ellis, somehow knowing that that image of him would stay with me and wanting to fix the details in my memory: the way his tightly curled hair stood out in sharp relief against the truck's reddish-brown door; the way he stood, leaning back, looking up, bad leg out to one side, weight on his cane; the easy grin that played across his face as he spoke, gesticulating, using his free hand to help his words along. I had never seen him so completely at ease, as unaffected as he appeared just then, and I felt a twinge of sadness, almost an envy.

Beside me Stacey said, 'Ellis,' with

resigned amusement, then after a moment added, 'I'm going to leave before he gets here.'

I glanced at her, saw that she was watching me, and turned to face her.

'We'll just argue,' she explained.

Stacey's dark eyes were strangely uncertain.

'I'll call,' she said, and started to move away.

I put my hand on her forearm and stopped her, looking at her, not wanting her to leave so abruptly, with nothing between us expressed; but I did not know what to say to her, and after a moment I withdrew my hand.

Stacey looked at me—looked at me hard, as if making a point—until I looked away. Out of the corner of my eye I saw her pick up her purse from the desk where she had put it and leave straightaway, without looking back. The door closer made a soft hissing sigh as she left, then noiselessly pushed the door closed behind her. When I turned back to the window, Ellis, too, was gone, and the reddish-brown truck was rolling away, turning out of its place in the row.

* * *

Ellis surprised me when he entered, coming into the office by a side door I had not noticed; and he paused only long enough to look at me curiously before he started forward, hobbling past me to a door opposite the one that he had entered. I had only to reach out to open the door, and I did, holding it for him, waiting for him to pass, noticing as he did that he did not look well. Beneath his beard his complexion was pale, almost pasty. His cheeks were taut. There were dark circles beneath his eyes.

'You don't look so good,' I said to his back, following him.

'I don't feel so good,' he replied brusquely.

When the door closed behind us, the darkness was so complete, so *black*, I stopped immediately, waiting for my eyes to adjust, listening to Ellis's uneven steps in front of me. 'Have you seen a doctor?' I asked.

I heard Ellis stop and turn, and in the darkness I felt his presence, felt his gaze on me disconcertingly near.

When he did not reply, I added, 'If you're worrying yourself sick, why don't you just give Esperoza back his sons?'

'I would if I had them, Tony,' he replied, his voice uncharacteristically subdued, 'but I don't.' A dim, red-yellow light came on, and I saw that we were in his darkroom, literally surrounded by the counters that ran along three walls and by the elaborate equipment set on top of them.

Ellis was propped against the work island in the middle of the room, arms crossed on his chest. 'I don't know where they are.

'Right,' I said skeptically, and looked around, annoyed, momentarily wondering why he needed three different enlargers. Hung on the wall near my shoulder was a strange-looking thermometer. I examined it, then asked casually, 'What about the float? Why did you allow Stacey and DeLloyd to hold up the collections? Or didn't you know about that, either?'

Ellis was looking directly at me.

'I knew,' he said flatly, his eyes hard and unmoving, 'and I knew it was a mistake.' He scratched his beard irritably, using his knuckles. 'But we had to try it. We needed the money.'

I thought about that as he turned away from me, moving to the counter on his left; I remembered what Stacey had said about the money, that it was still going down to Central America but that it was no longer coming back up.

'Needed the money for what?' I asked.

Ellis did not answer my question but lifted a large plastic tray instead, moving it slightly, just enough to ripple the clear liquid it contained. He semed so absorbed with what he was doing that for a moment I did not disturb him; then I realized what he had just admitted, and I said in disbelief, 'You were making money from the float? From DeLloyd's sleazy deals?'

With one finger Ellis touched the liquid in the tray, touched that finger to his tongue, said, 'I'm going to make some prints,' evasively, and turned away from me again.

'It isn't a float at all,' I concluded, making the obvious leap, another conclusion coming quickly. 'You're making loans—a series of short-term loans.'

I tried to make that fit, rethinking what I knew, but my memory of events was overshadowed by my memory of the two people who had told me most about them: I pictured DeLloyd as he explained his part in the collections, his expression dead serious and determined as he said matter-of-factly, 'Sometimes you got to talk to the people, let them know you serious, let them know they going to pay, one way or the other'; and I remembered Skinny explaining the deal to me—the Tees-and-Blues, diethyl-methyl-something and a painkiller—and how as he spoke, his eyes glistening, flicking back and forth, I had wondered how my father had gotten so turned around, caught up in such meanness.

'Three quarters of a million dollars,' Skinny had unknowingly answered for me.

At the thought of Skinny and his rude nasal voice I remembered something else that he had said, and I realized how perceptive he had been because it led me to another leap, this one much more important than the first, nearly incredible.

He had said, 'We're not talking drugs here, Curbel, we're talking *money*.'

We're talking money.

I said to Ellis softly, 'It *was* you. It was *your* money. You financed one of DeLloyd's sleazy deals, and you set me up when the marijuana was found on the boat, in with my mahogany. You and Dad set me up. You sent me to jail. To protect the money and your way of laundering it.'

Ellis glanced at me out of the corners of his eyes, then shook his head slowly from side to side.

'No,' he said, his voice low.

'You bastards,' I said, not willing to hear his excuses, stunned by the certainty of my own conclusion, feeling a coldness come over me, a hollowness. 'You low, conniving bastards.'

Ellis tiredly ran one hand over his face, pulling the skin taut.

'Not to protect the money, Tony,' he said, looking straight ahead, at the black-painted wall. 'To protect the plantation.' He turned to face me. 'To protect Mochita.'

At some place deep within myself I saw how obvious it had been all along—and I saw how hard I had worked not to believe it.

'You sent me to jail,' I repeated, remembering first how my father had told me that the money was not his, then how Ellis had told me that I had gone to jail because I was stupid.

I had worked so hard not to believe it, and even now, confronted by Ellis's admission, I could not fully grasp all that it meant.

'Mochita is bankrupt,' Ellis went on, as if that explained it all, his voice getting stronger, 'worse than bankrupt, sold out.'

Sold out, I thought, wondering if he knew what that really meant, how it felt; picturing my cell, remembering the indignities I had suffered, the assumptions I had made in their behalf because I had refused to believe that my father and my uncle would have put me there.

I had refused to believe it because I could not admit to myself that I could mean so little to them, to those who meant the most to me.

'My older brothers have been selling it off, piece by piece.'

I had loved them both, and they had used me.

'Why?' I asked, then stopped, suddenly unable to complete the question, unable to add, 'Why would you send me away?'

'Because they've been spending so extravagantly they can't pay their bills.'

'Not that,' I said, for some reason thinking just then of my mother, feeling the loss of her, the great sadness her death had brought, knowing somehow that this had begun then, when I was four years old. 'Not that.'

I slapped the wall once, hard.

'Not that,' I said again.

'We didn't have any choice,' Ellis said softly. 'We needed the money to buy up what they sold.'

I turned away from him, wanting to leave but knowing that I could not, not yet.

'We had to save the land, Tony. We had to. It's all we have.'

'Fuck you. Fuck your land.'

Ellis stepped in close behind me. I wheeled about to face him.

'I do not deserve this,' I said vehemently, the words spaced apart and distinct, pounding my fist in the air. 'I do not deserve it.'

Ellis put his big hands on my shoulders, squeezing tightly and looking down at me, his face near mine.

'*Our* land, Tony. It's our land. Your father and I are now the sixth generation; you will be the seventh. You think you're the first to pay a price for it? Our whole family has lived and died for that land—'

'*I* won't. *I* won't.' I turned away from him violently, twisting out of his grip. I slapped the wall again. 'I'll sell it like that—faster than that.'

'No,' Ellis said quietly, 'you won't. You can't, Tony. You couldn't even if you wanted to—it's too much a part of you.'

'I wasn't raised there, Ellis. It doesn't mean that much to me.'

‘You’re wrong about that, and you know it.’

Ellis was just standing there, looking at me, his expression concerned but maddeningly composed.

‘You think you know me so fucking well, but you don’t know me at all. Not at all. What gives you the right to interfere in my life?’ I pointed directly at him. ‘What price have you ever paid for the land?’

Just for a moment he seemed off balance; he looked away from me, then back.

‘I was sent away from it, Tony,’ he replied softly. ‘I know what it’s worth.’

I waved one hand disgustedly.

‘Poor, pitiful Ellis—’ I began.

‘Your mother is buried there,’ Ellis said flatly, brutally. ‘Your mother and your wife.’

I felt a cold deep anger rise in me, an outrage that he would use those deaths against me.

‘The land is all we’ve ever had that makes us special. We assume it, and we assume responsibility for it—for the dead who are buried there and for the living who work it. We’re responsible for them all. Whatever the cost.’

I knew what he was doing, how he was forcing me to confront the depth of my own emotion, evoking the bond between us—between all of us—and as he continued, his words droning, sounds, not really understood, I hated him for it. I hated his duplicity and his cruelty, his self-serving displays of concern. I hated his certainty, his inflated righteousness, his pride. I hated the sway that he held over me.

'It's our heritage, our name. Your father and I will be buried there, too.'

I felt the big muscles bunch in my shoulders, and when the door to the darkroom opened, I stepped toward it instinctively, moving to the light, away from him, because I knew I had to leave, knew a blind rage was taking me, becoming as uncontrollable as it had been when I was a boy, but much worse now, more frightening.

Back-lit, peering into the darkness, was the same solid man who the day before had moved toward me with purpose, his eyes fixed on my face, clutching a short, dull silver baseball bat. I saw the swelling on his cheek and the huge blue-black bruise around the eye; and as I stepped into the light, surprising him, I hit him, unhesitatingly, my full weight behind my fist, aiming for that same eye, feeling the rage inside me releasing, my hand connecting solidly, his head snapping to one side. Next to him I saw his partner, the compact man, his long-barreled revolver not held down this time but up, at arm's length.

A door burst open.

Someone shouted, 'Freeze motherfucker!' and I grabbed that arm just then, twisting it brutally, hearing the revolver explode into the darkroom before I felt a bone snap and the compact man sagged.

I twisted the arm further and kicked him away.

Against the desk there was a third man, moving back, fear and surprise registering on his round, clean-shaven face.

'I just want my sons,' he said, his soft brown eyes wide. 'I just want my sons.'

I grabbed his tie and hit him once, holding him close, hitting him again as he fell. And again.

'I want my father,' I screamed, smashing his face, smashing his nose flat, then working on one eye. 'I want my father. You give me back my father.'

I heard someone say, 'Jesus fucking Christ, Curbel,' and felt a heavy blow against my ribs.

I rolled away from the kick, coming up fast, one arm pressed against my side.

I saw a flash of silver head high and felt a sharp, hard jolt that stunned me, dropping me to my knees.

'He's a fucking banker, man. You'll kill the poor bastard.'

I moved forward, one hand drawing back; I saw a flash of silver again, just in front of me.

'Skinny ain't no banker, that's for sure.'

I looked up, into Skinny's hard, ferretlike eyes.

‘Back off,’ he said, cocking his silver revolver, aiming it low, at my knee, ‘or you’re down for the count. And then some.’

I felt my eyes go wide, calculating distance, flicking back and forth; and in that hesitation I felt a sag, a flat spot inside me. I sat back on my heels, the fury subsiding. I realized I was breathing heavily, my chest heaving.

Skinny said, ‘Christ, Curbel, you get excited, you go kind of fucking nuts, you know that?’

I did not reply to him but looked round instead, seeing first the solid man, face down, unconscious beside the door, then the compact man, on his side, holding his badly broken arm and moaning softly.

Skinny bent down and picked up the revolver that had fallen to the floor.

‘In case you didn’t catch his name,’ he said, standing up straight, gesturing to the third man by pointing the revolver, ‘that’s Esperoza.’ He held the long-barreled revolver up high and examined it. ‘Nice gun,’ he said. ‘Skinny might keep it.’ He grinned at me, then added, ‘These morons were watching your uncle. They probably figured you’d show up sooner or later—what they didn’t figure was that Skinny was watching *you*. The dumb bastards never even looked behind ’em.’

Just in front of me, Señor Esperoza was lying full length, both hands pressed to his face, holding his nose and eye. Blood had spattered on his shirt; his tie was pulled to one side and wrinkled. A slight paunch spilled around his middle, and beneath his hands his slack jowls pressed out loosely. From his soft shape alone it was easy to picture him in his bank, behind his big desk, his desk top gleaming beneath the papers that were there, smiling affably as he offered advice or nodding attentively, seriously, as he considered a request. His wavy black hair was tinged with gray, close-trimmed on the sides, thinning on top.

'I just want my sons,' he had said, and I believed him.

I ran one hand over my face, only then feeling the lump rising where Skinny had clubbed me with his revolver.

'Sorry about that,' Skinny said, seeing me feel my cheek. He raised and dropped both shoulders at once, flapping his arms in his peculiar way, only partially hiding his smug unconcern. He looked around, then asked, 'Where's your uncle, anyway? Weren't you with him?'

I rose to my feet, alarmed, moving quickly back to the darkroom, knowing Ellis would have been right behind me in a fight; then surprised to see that he was just where I had left him, having only taken a step or two back and propped himself against the counter.

'Are you okay?' he asked.

'Yes,' I replied, seeing that there was something unusual about the way he was standing, very nearly upright, with too much weight on his bad leg. Impatiently I waited for my eyes to adjust to the dim light so that I could see more clearly.

Behind me Skinny said, 'It's dark as shit in here.'

Ellis said to me, 'You're a mess.'

'I've been better,' I admitted, moving closer, seeing then that Ellis was holding his side, his big hand pressed against his ribs, and seeing the blood that had trickled between his fingers.

I said to Skinny, 'Call an ambulance. He's been shot.

Ellis protested, 'It's not that bad.'

'Then it won't take too long to fix,' I said, looking over my shoulder, motioning Skinny back.

Skinny turned and left, moving quickly.

'Who is that? Ellis asked. 'Is he the one who shot me?'

I shook my head.

'Esperoza,' I said softly. 'One of Esperoza's men shot you.'

'I'll be damned,' Ellis said, and pushed back against the counter, grimacing as he changed position slightly. 'I didn't think he had it in him.'

'It wasn't intentional,' I explained, then asked, 'Don't you want to sit down?'

'I'm fine where I am,' Ellis replied gruffly.

I saw an old towel on one of the counters and picked it up, smelling it and smelling darkroom chemicals on it before I folded it into a pad. Ellis accepted it reluctantly but finally put it under his hand, against his side.

Skinny shouted from the door. 'The ambulance will take about fifteen minutes to get here. How bad is it? Do you want to go in Skinny's car?'

Ellis said, 'I can wait.'

'It doesn't seem that bad,' I said, then added, 'Keep an eye on Esperoza.'

Skinny said sourly, 'No shit, Curbel.'

Ellis's expression was questioning, so I explained, 'That's the policeman who got me out of jail.'

Ellis pressed his lips together and looked straight ahead, watching Skinny leave. For a moment he seemed oblivious of me, and I examined the jagged small cuts on my knuckles. When I looked up, I saw that he was watching me.

'You've changed, Tony,' he said, his eyes assessing and thoughtful. 'You've changed quite a bit since you used to come to see me.'

'How is that?' I asked dutifully, only half-listening but wanting to remain nearby, in case he started to fall.

For a long moment Ellis was quiet, then he said, 'You used to ask questions. You used to want to know things.'

I shrugged noncommittally.

'It costs too much to know things.'

Ellis smiled at that, obviously pleased, and his smile surprised me.

'Yes,' he agreed idly, looking around before his eyes came back to me. 'It costs a lot.'

His eyes slid off me and he moved just slightly, shifting himself against the counter to relieve the weight on his arm. He seemed to be thinking over what he wanted to say next, and that, coupled with the apparent randomness of his observation, made it clear that he was about to begin a story.

I shifted my stance, too, pointedly making myself comfortable, waiting.

Ellis saw what I was doing—how I was gently poking fun at him by mimicking his preparation—and he said, 'One thing about you hasn't changed: you're still a smart ass.'

But he said it in a friendly, almost fond manner that was followed by a smile.

I shrugged again, smiling too.

Ellis looked past me, over me, at some point on the wall.

'I guess there's no stopping you,' I said.

He shot me an irritated glance.

'This one will cost you plenty,' he said, not so friendly now.

He took the towel from his side, looked at it, put it back.

'After the surgery on my leg,' he began, his

tone stubbornly insistent, 'as soon as I could travel, your grandmother took me to Mochita to recuperate. She's a very sharp woman, Tony, and very wise—don't ever underestimate her. She realized long before I did that I would have more problems with my head than with my leg, and she wanted me near her, just in case. The problem was, I had always been so healthy. I was as strong as an ox—nearly as big as one—and before I caught the polio I hadn't caught anything, ever, not even a cold. The polio affronted me. I didn't know how to deal with it, and Mother knew I would learn to walk again long before I would adjust to being a gimp.'

Ellis glanced at me out of the corners of his eyes.

'I wasted years letting my own anger consume me.'

That message to me was too direct for Ellis and made him uncomfortable; he looked up at the ceiling, then went on quickly, 'My two older brothers—the uncles you hardly know—were a good deal more arrogant back then. They made it a point to let me know they didn't like having me around, crippled or otherwise; but to kick me out they would have had to get past your grandmother—and they knew better than to try.

'Anyway, after a time, after about three or four months, I suppose, I was able to get around on my own. I had to use crutches, and it was tough: I have a lot of weight to carry. But I wanted out of that house, so I took to fishing the river, and every afternoon I made my way down to the little pier, took the boat and floated down to the gravel bar where the river turns—'

'I know the place,' I interrupted him, pleased despite myself, pleased by my memory: during my summer in Mochita I had stopped on that gravel bar in the evenings, hot and sweaty after a day spent exploring, and I had lain full length on the cool gravel, putting my face in the water and drinking deeply, tasting the minerals, resting before I went on to the house. I remembered the way the late afternoon light had played across the river, golden and silvery on the babbling water, and how it was dark beneath the arching banks. 'On the upstream side the gravel comes out'—I held up a bent finger—'and makes a little peninsula.'

'That's it.' Ellis nodded, the brief shadow of a smile flickering across his face. 'That's it.'

Again he took the towel from his side and looked at it, but this time, instead of putting it back, he threw it into the sink with the pan he used for washing prints.

'See,' he went on, before I could protest, 'I took the boat because I could hardly carry myself, much less my equipment; and I stopped on the gravel bar because it was easy to get out there and it wasn't too far for my nurse to walk—she came down from the house with my pole and tackle box.' He shrugged, jerking his head to one side. 'Later she brought tortillas, a few bottles of beer . . .'

Ellis went off somewhere in his mind, replaying those afternoons, but after a moment he said, his voice very low, 'Even today, Tony, I'm not sure what I had in mind: I'm not sure if I really just wanted out of the house or if I just wanted to see her alone.'

'To see who alone?' I asked, fairly certain that I understood him but wanting to be sure. 'Your nurse?'

'My nurse,' Ellis affirmed. He gave me a quick, hard look. 'Stacey Veldran's mother.'

'Her mother?' I asked dumbly, and that quickly I understood why I had never met Stacey before, why I had never heard her name mentioned, not once, not even in passing: in Central America a child born out of wedlock is considered something less than human by *respectable* families, something never spoken about, never acknowledged in even the smallest way.

'When I found out she was pregnant I wanted to marry her, but your grandmother got to her first: my mother called her into her study one afternoon, and after that she disappeared. I didn't hear from her or see her for almost ten years . . .'

'Until after her husband was killed,' I concluded for him, remembering what Stacey had told me when I had first met her.

Ellis's face registered a mild surprise that passed quickly.

'Right,' he said softly. 'That's when she asked me to see to Stacey's education, and I brought Stacey up here, to the States.'

I rubbed my chin thoughtfully, suddenly feeling very sorry for Stacey, understanding her much better, understanding her insularity, her barely concealed resentment.

'Does she know?' I asked, and immediately I saw that I had hit at the core of what Ellis was telling me. It was in the way his eyes filled with regret, then slipped away from me: that furtive glance revealed that he had never admitted it to her, not directly. Yet after all these years certainly Stacey had to have figured out why Ellis had taken her in. She had to know that Ellis was her father—and Ellis knew that she knew—but it had remained unsaid between them.

'Why didn't you ever tell her?' I asked, but before Ellis could reply, Skinny appeared in the doorway, a lanky, intrusive shadow against the bright light behind him.

'The ambulance is here,' Skinny announced. 'It just pulled into the lot.' He looked over his shoulder, then back. 'Skinny hopes to shit he can walk,' he added sourly. 'It's two women paramedics—they couldn't move him with a hand truck.'

Moving very cautiously, Ellis pushed himself away from the counter. He looked down at his hand before he looked back at me. 'I had to tell you,' he said. 'You had to know.'

In the office I heard a loud knocking, and I glanced away from him, to the door, and saw Skinny rapping on the window, waving rudely to the paramedics.

I felt Ellis's hand on my shoulder.

'You had to know to find Carl,' he said, and moved past me, reaching for his cane in the corner where he had left it. 'You had to know,' he repeated, as if affirming it to himself. 'If Stacey had had *her* father, none of this would have happened.'

CHAPTER ELEVEN

The two women paramedics worked very purposefully and very efficiently, and despite Skinny's doubts, easily loaded both Ellis and the compact man into the ambulance. Skinny called for a police car to transport the solid man and Señor Esperoza, and just as the ambulance left the huge parking lot, the police car arrived, its blue lights flashing and its tires squealing as it moved quickly between two rows of trucks.

The small crowd of truckers that had formed dispersed, the truckers walking away with exaggerated casualness, singly or in pairs, back to their trucks or back to the twenty-four-hour restaurant.

Skinny conferred briefly with the two uniformed policemen, gave instructions, and went back into the office; after a few minutes he reappeared with Señor Esperoza and the solid man both following him. The solid man moved very hesitantly, still dazed, his cheek swollen even larger. Señor Esperoza held a blood-spotted handkerchief to his nose and eye; standing up, he appeared to be even more the banker that he was, his round, solid shape, conservative suit, and dark tie combining to give the impression of substance and reliability.

When I walked up to him he did not seem to recognize me until I said, '*Le regresaré sus hijos*' (I will get you back your sons); then he turned to me and studied me with the dark brown eye that was not covered.

He replied only, 'Your father is well,' and walked on, going to the police car and sitting in the back seat, leaving the door open, looking straight ahead.

Behind me the policemen laughed, and I glanced back in time to see Skinny laughing with them, finishing a joke, embellishing it with gestures.

Señor Esperoza sat very still, sitting up

straight on the seat, looking straight ahead.

I turned around and leaned back against the police car, looking down, waiting. For a moment I thought about Stacey Veldran, picturing her as she had awakened that morning, pulling the sheet up around herself, then remembering the way she had looked at me before she had left the truck stop's office, her eyes very hard, making a point—and making no secret of the fact that she was avoiding Ellis. And I thought about the relationship between Ellis and her, wondering what Ellis had thought, at about the same age I was now, suddenly given the responsibilities of being a father. I wondered where Stacey had lived, where she had gone to school, what she had thought, forced to adapt to a new language and new customs, to a gruff new father who very likely was just as confused as she.

On the sidewalk in front of me I saw Skinny's grimy canvas boots. I looked up and stepped away from the fender against which I had been leaning.

Skinny said, 'How about some breakfast, Curbel? Skinny's so hungry he could eat a horse.'

I watched the police car leave, going back the way it had come, between two rows of trucks; then I followed Skinny around the outside of the building, remembering the two times in less than a day that I had followed him before: once down the French Market, past the displays of produce, and once through the prison's noisy hallways.

* * *

Heads turned as we entered the twenty-four-hour restaurant, and curious eyes followed us to the booth that Skinny chose. I sat down quickly, pretending not to notice, but Skinny remained standing, enjoying the attention, looking around and smiling as the waitress removed the dirty dishes and wiped the table with a rag.

Before he sat down Skinny ran both hands through his hair; before he picked up the plastic-covered menu the waitress left he wiped his hands on the legs of his jeans.

He glanced at the menu, said to me excitedly. 'Man, they even got your kind of food here, Curbel: they got nachos,' and looked at the menu again.

I took a paper napkin from the dispenser and wiped the damp table in front of me.

The waitress brought us each a cup of coffee, took an order pad from her apron pocket, and asked, 'What can I do for you this morning?'

Skinny smiled lewdly, looking her up and down. 'Sweetheart,' he began, but she stopped him with an impatient glance. Skinny shrugged and ordered an omelet; I asked for biscuits and milk.

'So, Curbel,' Skinny began after the waitress had left, pushing his coffee to one side, leaning forward, 'did you get a look at the books?'

I sat back in the booth, away from him, and idly stirred my coffee, looking at the spoon.

'No,' I lied, preferring not to have to explain that I had seen the books but had not been able to read them. 'Stacey was about to show them to me, but she never got to it—'

'Yeah?' he asked rudely, putting both hands on his chest and moving them up and down. 'Something get in the way?'

I removed the spoon from the coffee.

'Someone shot out the windows in her den.'

Skinny sat back in the booth and ran one hand across his face, feeling his two-day stubble with his fingers, scraping it.

'Yeah?' he asked again, but thoughtfully this time. 'Did you call the police?'

I nodded, watching as he reached for the stainless steel-topped bowl of sugar and flipped it open.

'Skinny'll get the report,' he said absently. He picked up the spoon that had been left with his coffee, dipped it into the sugar, scooped out a heaping teaspoonful. 'Skinny doesn't much believe in coincidence, Curbel,' he said, and rather than put the sugar in his coffee, he brought it to his mouth and ate it, sucking and chewing it simultaneously.

'So?' I said noncommittally, knowing what he was getting at but waiting to see how he would figure it.

'So,' he replied, swallowing hurriedly, 'you ask to see the books, you get shot at—you think that's an accident?'

'Esperoza has already—' I began.

'Think, Curbel.' Skinny cut me off, tapping the spoon against his forehead, jerking forward so that he seemed about to come across the table. 'How did you get to her house?'

I did not care to hold his harsh gaze, and I turned my head to look out at the cars and trucks speeding past on the highway, recalling as I did so the walk I had taken from the French Quarter to the Garden District, realizing the obvious conclusion: that if Esperoza had been following me he would have taken me then, during that walk. He would not have waited to shoot out a window—and if he hadn't been following me he would not have known where I was. But there was something too pat about that conclusion, something that made me want to deny it.

I said, 'Stacey was standing right beside me when it happened.'

Skinny snorted disgustedly.

'Man, she doesn't have to pull the trigger

to do the shooting.' He started to reach again for the sugar but stopped halfway, his spoon poised in midair. 'What's the matter, Curbel? It hurts your feelings to think she would try to nail you?'

I thought about that for a moment, pursing my lips, allowing that it might; then I saw Skinny smile, genuinely amused.

'Shit, Curbel, Skinny can't believe it: you nailed *her*, didn't you?' His smile broadened. 'Son of a bitch. Skinny didn't think she'd put out at all—he didn't even try for it.' He shook his head, still smiling. 'Son of a bitch,' he said again.

That quickly the waitress came with our food, and Skinny sat back, his eyes following the plate she placed in front of him. As soon as she had gone for my milk he picked up the bottle of ketchup she had put on the table between us and began to pour it, a heavy thick layer of it, over his eggs, hash browns, and bacon.

'Skinny had her figured for it, Curbel,' he said, recapping the ketchup and putting it to one side. 'He just had her on a long leash so he could see what bushes she sniffed, see who'd been doing their business where.'

'Figured for what?' I asked, refusing to let him disturb me.

He did not reply because he had already taken a big bite of potatoes and was chewing, smacking his lips, a watery red froth forming at one corner of his mouth.

I cut a biscuit in half and buttered it, not looking up until he said, 'That Esperoza is a tough old bird.' He cut a piece from his omelet. 'No matter what Skinny said, he just kept asking for his lawyer.'

I had no trouble believing that but wondered about Skinny's apparent non sequitur, about how he would tie his last two observations together.

Skinny put the piece of omelet into his mouth, wiped his chin with the back of his hand, and said, 'With him out of the way, we'll nail her down tight, cut her off for about ten years.' He chewed thoughtfully, then added, 'Unless she likes girls.'

I opened the container of jelly that had come with my biscuits and cut out a small, pale square of it.

'Skinny still wants you to take a look at the books.'

I spread the jelly, put down the knife, picked up the crumbly biscuit; but when I opened my mouth to take a bite, I felt a deep, painful soreness in my jaw and returned it to the plate.

Skinny took it and took a big bite of it, smiling again. I pushed the plate across to him.

'First time around,' Skinny said, talking as he chewed, chopping off another piece of omelet, 'when Skinny sent you to see the books, he figured that whoever stopped you from seeing them was the one diddling with the money.' He paused to swallow and to wipe at the ketchup that had dribbled down his chin. 'That makes sense, right? Who else would care whether or not you saw them? That's why Skinny got you out of jail: not to see what you could find out but to see who would stop you when you started to poke around.' He grinned and shoveled the omelet into his mouth. 'You couldn't miss.'

I took another napkin from the dispenser, dipped it into my water, wiped it gently across my cheek.

'And whoever was diddling with the money was the one making the deal for the Tees-and-Blues—that makes sense, too, right? So now that we know the girl is good for it—'

'We don't know it,' I interrupted, though even as I denied it I was beginning to see how it might fit. 'Not for a fact.'

Skinny had started to put a piece of biscuit in his mouth, but he withdrew it and said sourly, 'We're not going to court here, Curbel. We're still working the case. There's a difference.' He put the piece of biscuit into his mouth.

I held my spoon with both hands and bent it, flexing the handle between my thumbs, thinking again of Stacey and of what Ellis had told me, that he was her father. And if that was true, I wondered, when had Stacey learned it and how had it affected her? How long had it been before resentment had begun to build in her? How long before that resentment had become hatred strong enough that she would want to destroy him, seeing his need to save Mochita and using it against him, striking at his weakness? That was what Ellis expected me to believe, wasn't it? That was why he had told me the story—another in a long line of stories—justifying himself, his refusal to fight back.

'So Skinny wants you to see the books for real this time,' he said after he had swallowed, 'see what's in 'em. The books will tie it all together—they'll show how your uncle and your father were right in there, too—and *that* we'll take to court.'

I thought about that for a moment, trying to picture Skinny in court, wondering how he would dress, whether or not he would wear his torn jeans and his sleeveless green fatigue jacket, and trying to hear how he would speak, whether or not he would curse so freely in front of a judge; then I realized what he had said, and I asked casually, acting perplexed, 'Right in where?' hoping my casualness would mask my anxiety.

Skinny snorted again, derisively, spraying small, soggy crumbs of biscuits.

'Right in there financing the deal, Curbel—principals to conspiracy to distribute a controlled dangerous substance.' He used his thumb to push the last of his potatoes onto his fork.

'I thought you were after the agency,' I said.

Skinny licked his thumb, ate the potatoes, and said, 'This is better,' as he picked up a ketchup-covered piece of bacon. 'Hit 'em with an illegal alien rap, and what? They pay a fine. Big deal. It's not worth Skinny's time to make the case. But we let the deal go through, we get 'em for the drugs, they do ten years. Ten years hard time. That's why Skinny cut Lips loose: to let him close the deal.'

'You let Lips go?' I asked, only beginning to understand what he was up to but somehow fearing it already, knowing that Skinny was both clever and unpredictable, a very real threat.

'Yeah,' he replied, and tore the bacon with his teeth. 'To catch the fish you have to play out the line, Curbel. And you have to put a worm on the end of it. Make the hook look tasty.' He smiled as he chewed, obviously amused by his own analogy. 'Lips wet his pants he was so excited. He couldn't believe it. He gets to walk *and* to nail the people who put him into the trick in the first place. All he has to do is to set the deal and tell Skinny where it's going to happen. Skinny shows up with the troops. Nothing to it. With Esperoza out of the way, it won't take long, either.' He raised and dropped both shoulders at once. 'Maybe it'll happen tonight.'

Skinny pushed his plate to one side, picked up his cup of coffee, took a sip of it. For a long moment he just looked at me, his green-yellow eyes amused and smug.

A deep chill ran though me, a dread.

He is setting the deal, I thought, trying to order what he was telling me, *so that he can stop it as it happens.*

'Skinny's got the storehouse for the Tees,' he went on, his eyes still amused. 'He's got Lips. And he's got you, Curbel—he's never been so solid.'

Stacey, Ellis, my father, I thought, picturing each one in turn, *they are all so distracted by their own concerns they do not see what is happening to them all, the trap they have set for themselves.*

'The books are the icing, Curbel,' Skinny continued. He emptied his cup of coffee in one long pull, noisily rinsed it around his mouth, swallowed it, and shrugged. 'He could probably work around 'em, but he wants 'em.'

They are all linked together, and that is the real danger: not that the money and the plantation will be lost but that if the deal takes place, they will all go to prison.

'You find the books,' Skinny said, sitting forward, his eyes no longer amused but in a blink, very suddenly, very hard, 'and you get them to Skinny. You got that?'

They will all go to prison—not to jail for a year or two, which is bad enough—but to prison for ten years. Ten years hard time.

'You got that?' Skinny repeated. 'You try to hold out, Curbel, and you're back in the joint yourself—that Skinny guarantees.'

And it will all be lost. All of it. What family I have. The land. The money.

'But that's up to you,' Skinny said dismissively. 'Just like before.'

He picked up the paper napkin I had put down and wiped his mouth as he stood up.

'But if Skinny were you, Curbel,' he said down to me, 'he'd stick it to 'em, just like they stuck him.'

I cannot allow it to happen, I thought, feeling a sinking dread, a fear that began in my chest.

Skinny ran his fingers under the lapel of my jacket, idly feeling the material, pinching it between his greasy thumb and first finger.

'Nice coat,' he said, smiling coyly, coldly. 'Is that the one you had in the property room?'

I cannot allow it, I thought again, feeling the dread and the fear intermixing, not knowing how I could prevent it but knowing that I had to find a way. I had underestimated Skinny—I had thought I could say one thing and do another—and now he was calling me on it, forcing my hand.

'The little wheels are turning, eh, Curbel?' Skinny said.

The waitress came up beside him.

'Anything else?' she asked, writing on her order pad, not looking up.

'You got any toothpicks?' Skinny asked.

She handed him the check, and he took it.

'By the cash register,' she said, and moved away.

Skinny looked at the check, then put it down on the table.

'Get this, will you, Curbel: Skinny's a little short.' He wiped his mouth again, then tossed the wadded napkin onto the table. 'Skinny'll get his car and meet you in front.'

He left the table, stopped at the cash register, and went out through the glass door; and I stared after him, watching his jerky movements, his overlong strides, for some reason remembering just then the old trusty in the property room, the way he had blown the dust off the package that held my clothes.

'You never forget the first time you get out,' the old man had said. 'Never.'

As I stood up I bumped into the waitress; she smiled wanly, tiredly, stepped back, and waited for me to pass.

CHAPTER TWELVE

Skinny had driven very fast, recklessly, weaving at high speed in and out of traffic from the time we had left the truck stop until we had reached the Garden District; and he had left his window open so that the wind and the noise had roared through the car the whole way except when he had taken a portable radio from beneath the seat and had spoken into it: then he had rolled the window up and had slowed the car considerably as he had reported in, speaking in a technical-sounding jargon that contained as many numbers as words. As soon as he had switched the radio off, however, he had rolled the window back down and had speeded back up, neither speaking to me nor looking at me, not acknowledging me in any way until he had stopped a few blocks from Stacey Veldran's house, reached across my lap and pushed open the door—and then he had said only, 'Get those books, Curbel,' and had waited impatiently for me to get out, staring at me as if challenging me to reply.

I had gotten out of the car deliberately slowly, and he had raced off even before I had turned around, allowing the car's jump forward to slam shut the door; and once again I found myself walking to Stacey's house, walking in the street, staying off of the uneven sidewalks that had been broken by the roots of trees.

As I approached the house, instead of going straight to the front, I went around back and stood near the opening in the thick hedges, leaning on the low chain-link gate, looking up at an angle, studying the two broken windows fifty feet away.

Standing exactly where whoever had shot out the windows had stood, I could almost feel the long, solid weight of a rifle in my hands—the way the hard ridge of the stock pressed against your cheek, how the butt pressed into the hollow of your shoulder—and it was easy to picture Stacey and me in the den, moving about just before the bullets smashed through the glass. I pictured the soft yellow light from the table lamp. Stacey in her white, thigh-length bathrobe, me, my back to the window, weight on one foot, one hand in my pocket. And it was easy to picture us not just then but earlier in the evening, too, when the projector's intense white light had flashed surreally, when I had reached through the space of harsh light between us and pulled her blouse aside, when in my head I had heard the screams I had heard in jail at night and the baleful, wounded-animal whimpering that had followed . . .

I regretted the way that Stacey and I had

begun, each using the other, and looking at those two shattered windows, I recalled thinking of my wife, realizing how much I still missed her. Just for a moment I had to question how much one was related to the other—how the loss of one had led to the calculated use of the other. That use, I supposed, was what had brought the screams in my head, the realization that I was not so different from the tattooed biker I had fought. And it did not help when, after a while, I saw that in very different ways both Ellis and Skinny had reached the same conclusion: Stacey had been using us all. In one way I hoped they were right because, if they were, it meant that while my father had sent me to jail, he had not set me up to go to jail, a very significant distinction; yet in another way I felt the opposite, hoping they were wrong so that I could tell myself there had been, at least, some feeling.

I put both hands on top of the gate and squeezed the metal tightly, twisting my wrists until the cords that ran through them pulled painfully taut. I felt a bitter disgust that we had all so blatantly set out to use each other, but I knew I could not then afford the anger resentment would bring. I released my grip and just stood there until the taut pain in my wrists receded.

A car passed on the street behind me.

I listened to it until it was gone, then left

my spot at the gate, went around to the front of the house, up the walk, up the stairs, across the porch.

I rang the bell and waited, looking back at the quiet street, down on it, over the hedges. When no one answered I peered in through the cut glass in the door and saw that the house appeared empty and undisturbed. I tried the door, but it was locked. Uncertain what to do next, I walked down the porch, opened the heavy dark green shutters, and peered in again from a different angle, cupping my hands against the glass in the walk-through, double-hung windows. Inside I saw the yarn the policemen had stretched to trace the path of the bullets, still in place, still running room-to-room through the walls. In the dim interior light the yarn was not so bright as I remembered it. It sagged slightly now, limp and somehow lifeless.

The window slid up.

Startled, I jerked back, looking to see who had raised it, and I saw DeLloyd Lincoln standing to one side of the window frame, looking out at me, his dark suit and darker face seeming to come out of the low light behind him.

'You here, you might as well come in,' he said, and raised the window higher.

I stepped through the window, and he closed it, then turned to face me, his brown-black eyes moving over me with casual assurance and confidence before he caught my gaze and held it.

'You seen Stacey?' he asked, and just as when I had met him previously, in my apartment, I was struck by the sheer size of him, by his massive, threatening presence.

'I saw her earlier,' I said. 'This morning.'

He looked at the window, twisted the lock, and looked back at me.

'What happen to your face?' he asked.

Automatically, I reached up and touched my cheek, probing the swelling with my fingertips.

'Skinny,' I replied, moving my jaw from side to side, feeling the same deep soreness I had felt at breakfast.

DeLloyd's impatience passed in a dark cloud across his face, and I realized that he did not know Skinny.

'Señor Esperoza and his two helpers,' I explained. 'The two you put in my tub.'

'You catch up to them or the other way 'round?'

'A bit of both,' I said, forcing a thin smile.

'You get your father back?'

'No,' I replied evenly.

DeLloyd responded to my reply by allowing his eyes to droop, looking at me curiously, assessingly.

After a moment he said, 'I makin' coffee,' and abruptly moved past me, walking down the center hallway, toward the kitchen.

I adjusted my jacket and followed him, smoothing my tie, pinching my collar around the knot, admiring the fluid grace of his movements, his ominous ease.

In the kitchen, the coffee cups Stacey and I had used the night before were just where we had left them on the counter. I took them to the sink and rinsed them as DeLloyd finished making the coffee. We both leaned back against a counter—DeLloyd against the counter on the window wall, I against the counter beside the sink—so that we stood at a right angle to each other; and we both idly watched the glass coffeepot fill, listening to the coffeemaker gurgle and hiss.

Finally, DeLloyd looked back at me and asked, 'Stacey say where she was going?'

I shook my head from side to side, and said, 'No,' as I slowly shifted my eyes to his. 'But she did say you might be the one who shot at us last night.'

DeLloyd didn't even blink. His eyes drooped again, assessingly, pensively, and he crossed his thick arms on his chest.

'Maybe,' he said. 'Maybe she the one told me to do it, too. Maybe she think she need to run you off, think you going to be a problem.' He spread his big hand on his upper arm and absently rubbed his bicep.

'What kind of a problem?' I asked.

'What you think, man?' he snapped. 'We only got one thing working.'

I thought about that for a moment, trying to understand exactly what he was telling me—and trying to understand, too, why he was telling me anything at all.

'Why—' I began, but before I could finish my question, before I could say. 'Why would you need to run me off?' DeLloyd broke in, ''Cause last night I so low I feel lucky if I back parking cars at the Monteleone garage.' He uncrossed his arms and put both hands down flat on the counter. 'I figure I ain't got no choice but do what she say. I figure I got to stay in the game—got to see what happen.'

DeLloyd paused. A green vein pulsed in his temple.

'Later on, the score change. I get lucky.'

'The coffee's done,' I said, looking away from him, knowing immediately how the score had changed and giving myself time to think.

DeLloyd glanced over his shoulder, then turned back to the counter. He allowed the last few drops to drip from the coffeemaker before he picked up the pot and filled the cups I had rinsed. He replaced the pot, added sugar to both cups, turned back, and held one out to me.

'Got to drink it black,' he said as I stepped forward to accept it. 'She out of milk.'

I tasted the coffee, stepped back to the sink, sipped again. Skinny had told me that he had released Lips the night before, and when DeLloyd had said, 'Later on, the score change,' I knew immediately that Lips must have gone straight to DeLloyd, offering to close the deal for the Tees-and-Blues. What I did not know was how to play it, how to use to best advantage the fact that Lips was Skinny's bait.

'So you caught up to Lips?' I asked casually, looking at DeLloyd over the rim of my cup, smiling easily. 'Did you break his nappy head?'

DeLloyd's face registered mild surprise, then irritation. His round, black nostrils flared, making his nose appear even flatter, and his upper lip curled back in an ugly sneer. He looked at his coffee, then at me; after a moment he dropped his glance to the floor, his expression softening, becoming troubled and speculative.

'Your uncle,' he said, 'he straight with me from the start—he the only white man I ever knew that treat me right. I don't trust the man at first, him and his welfare-looking beauty parlor, got money but drive a raggedy old car, sleep on a fold-out couch—act like he hiding something.' DeLloyd tilted his coffee back toward himself and looked at it again. 'But the man always back up what he say, make it good, so what I care where he sleep? He make me go to school, make me learn to read and write.' He glanced up to look directly at me, his eyes hard and challenging;

when I looked away, he continued, 'So when he say he got to get his nephew out of jail no matter what he has to do, he need him out, I accept that; and when he say I got to help his nephew, got to be there for him, keep an eye on him, keep him out of the shit, I accept that, too—that's why I there when those two little fuckers break in your place with their baseball bat. Because your uncle sent me.'

'Because your uncle sent me,' he said, but his hard glance added, 'Not because you're worth it.'

'So when Stacey say scare you off, I figure maybe that the best thing. Do what she say. Keep you gone. Keep you out of the shit. Give me time to find Lips.'

DeLloyd moved his shoulders forward and back in an uncertain shrug. The corners of his mouth turned down.

'Later on, Lips catch up to me instead. And you still here, thinking you so smart.'

I held my coffee with both hands.

'Why did Stacey want to scare me off?' I asked.

DeLloyd made a derisive sound, a grunt that came through his nose.

'Same reason as me—I told you, we only got the one thing working.' He looked directly at me. 'Maybe she just don't like you, don't like you nosin' around, don't know who you working for, how you got yourself out of jail. It weren't for your uncle . . .' he began, then stopped himself, his words trailing off before his eyes came back to me. 'Something wrong between you and him. The man carry too much weight with you, worry too much about you.'

I shrugged that one off.

'Are you and Lips set to close the deal?' I asked.

DeLloyd gave me a long, cool look before he turned away, refilled his cup, turned back.

'Where is your uncle, anyway?' he asked, pointedly not replying to my question. 'I been trying to get him since early. He usually up.'

I turned my wrist to look at my watch, noting that it was nearly noon.

'Right about now,' I said, glancing back at DeLloyd, 'he should be going into surgery. He was shot.'

DeLloyd's eyes locked on mine.

'He shot bad?'

I shook my head.

'He'll be all right. He took one bullet'—I poked myself in the side—'right about here.'

DeLloyd put one hand on his hip, leaned to the same side, crossed his ankles. His eyes were troubled.

'That when that happen to your face? When he shot?'

I nodded.

'You sure he all right?'

I nodded again.

DeLloyd pressed his lips together tightly.

He shook his head slowly, side to side; then without warning he slapped the counter, hard, smacking his palm against the wood.

'Damn,' he said sharply, angrily. 'I should of drowned those two motherfuckers when they in the tub—had the chance and let it go.'

He said it more to himself than to me, a self-reproving edge on his words.

'Should of kept up with Lips from the start, none of this shit would of happen.'

He slapped the counter again, then after a moment turned away to face the window.

'I should of been there with your uncle, not out chasing after shit.'

I looked at his broad shoulders, seeing the intimidating power in them in the way they stretched his coat.

'He'll be all right,' I said again.

DeLloyd ran one finger along the windowsill, inspected the dust he had collected, irritably rubbed his thumb and that finger together.

'He must have wanted you where you were—'

'So what, what he want?' he snapped, wheeling around, turning back to me, his brown-black eyes hot and angry. 'What he want don't mean shit. The man ain't got no sense about himself. Got to treat him like a child, make him come in out the rain when he wet.'

DeLloyd started forward, realized he was

still holding his cup of coffee, threw the cup to one side, sliding it down the counter; then he left the kitchen, moving past me without a glance, moving down the center hallway, the sound of his steps hard and angry against the bare wood floor. I poured out the last of my coffee and rinsed the cup, then I retrieved his cup and rinsed it, too, putting both cups beside the sink to dry.

DeLloyd's anger lingered in the kitchen, an ugly, threatening energy in the air, and I hesitated before I followed him, wondering what it was I hoped to accomplish with him, trying to understand what there was about his anger that affected me so deeply, viscerally, giving me a sick, sinking feeling in my gut.

From a room down the hall came the muffled sound of a drawer slammed shut. Something heavy thumped.

And that readily, it was there, in those sounds and the ugly presence of unrestrained anger, the reason for that feeling. The memory came to me not as remembrances of separate days but as a composite, an image of myself as a boy—an image compounded from all the days I had lain on my bed in the late afternoon, head turned to one side, looking out the window at the soothing shades of green in the nearby plants and trees.

In my memory, blue-green holly is nearest, just beneath my window. Then there are light green vines on the fence, beyond which there are dark green oaks and magnolias. It is so quiet I can hear the pinging tick of my wrist watch. I can feel the vibration in my bones.

In the driveway a car door shuts; the door to the house slams closed. My heartbeat quickens. I strain to hear, to discern from the sounds—the weight of his steps, light or heavy; the pace of his movements, fast or slow—what sort of mood my father is in, what sort of evening it is likely to be.

He has made the bedroom across from mine his study, and now he is there, opening his mail, reading it, stapling papers together, opening and closing the big drawer in his desk.

He curses in Spanish. The trash can bangs. Kicked across the room, it hits the wall and clatters to the floor.

I feel a tightness in my gut.

It is bad.

I hear his steps approaching, his heavy, thick-soled shoes slapping the floor as he moves, hard and very angry.

I feel a sick, sinking feeling, a morbid dread not helped by my certain knowledge that just through the wall, in the room next to mine, my sister is listening as I am listening, ears straining to catch each nuance of every sound, trying to read those same fearsome vibrations in the air, dread-filled as I am dread-filled, waiting.

What was he thinking then, I wondered,

when he came home like that, day after day? Or did he even know how we cowered when he entered? Was he so caught up in himself and his own affairs that he did not know that our whole lives were determined by his moods? Did he ever consider, even once, the fear we felt when the rage took him? Or did he know how we hated those long, anxiety-filled dinners as we listened to his knife and fork tap against his plate, endured his venomous looks, and when another mood took him, his acid, cutting diatribes directed against all those who were conspiring to keep him from success? It wasn't until years later—until after I had married and had observed my wife's strong effect on me—that I began to understand what a difference my mother's presence would have made. I began to see how another adult would have moderated the unbridled force of his moods. But as children, my sister and I knew only that we had to endure because there was no other option open to us. We were helpless, and in the irrational way of children, deep within ourselves we felt we deserved it—we were, as we were told so often, worthless. Events had proved without doubt that message our father repeated: we were, in fact, so worthless that our own mother had left us. She was gone, forever, and that was proof enough.

I crossed my arms on my chest, looked

down, then up.

I heard DeLloyd mumbling to himself, and I heard his determined footsteps in the hall, moving toward the den.

In the window over the sink I caught a glimpse of myself, a shadowy reflection.

'Is that it, buddy?' I asked myself, catching a gleam in my own eyes, a spark. 'That's all the problem you got?'

I cocked my head to one side, turned away from the window.

You get your father back, I thought, *and you keep him out of jail.*

I went into the den to see what DeLloyd was doing.

⋆ ⋆ ⋆

DeLloyd was on his knees, opening and closing the cabinets beneath the bookcase, rummaging through them.

'Watch the glass,' I suggested, making my presence known, seeing on the floor, as he moved forward, several fragments from the windows.

He did not seem to hear me but ducked his head to look closely at a small box that he had found.

'What are you doing?' I asked curiously.

DeLloyd cradled the box in one big hand as he gently removed the top. He looked into the box, then at me, his eyes drooping again, a warning.

'What you care?' he said, then added, 'You going to try to stop me?'

Between him and me, beneath the table behind the couch, I saw the slide projector where Stacey had left it, balanced upright, and still attached to it the carousel of slides that she had shown me.

'I thought maybe I could help,' I said.

DeLloyd replaced the top on the box, put it back on the shelf where he had found it. As he continued his search I moved forward and casually lifted the projector onto the table. It took me a moment to figure out how to remove the tray from the projector, and in getting it off, two slides fell to the floor. I squatted down to pick him up, seeing as I did that one was a page from Stacey's illegible account books and the other was the picture of my father at his door.

DeLloyd moved on to another cabinet.

I removed the slides from the tray and put them in my pocket. DeLloyd did not seem to have noticed what I had done, and I stood up and returned the projector to the floor.

Finally he slammed shut the last cabinet and rose to his feet.

'I got to see Stacey or your uncle,' he said, 'one or the other.'

I did not speculate about why he might need to see them but looked at him blankly.

'I got to get in their box,' he explained, 'the

safety box they keep at the bank downtown.'

I thought about that for a moment, wondering what DeLloyd needed from the box and trying to remember whether or not Ellis had made me a signatory for it. I knew I could get into the box my father kept for the employment agency; if Ellis used the agency box as his own, I could get into it.

And Ellis is cheap, I thought, knowing that he would be unlikely to pay for a second box if he didn't have to.

'Why?' I asked DeLloyd, asking it casually, patting my pockets, feeling for my keys.

'It don't concern you,' he replied sullenly, and turned to face the windows.

As he moved forward, moved in front of the couch to the windows, and inspected the damage his bullets had done, I found my keys and took them out. Quietly I sorted through them, one at a time, careful not to jangle them on the ring, until I came to the flat key with the very square-cut notches, the key to the agency's safe deposit box.

DeLloyd said, 'I got to get in the box because that where your uncle keep his cash, the cash he got hid for tonight.' He reached up and tore off a long, splintered piece of sash.

'How much cash?' I asked.

DeLloyd rolled one shoulder forward and back in a glum, uncertain shrug. 'Don't matter, I can't get at it,' he said. He turned the splinter over and back, examining it.

Even before I said, 'I can get in the box,' I knew what I was going to do and what it would cost DeLloyd when I did it.

'Ten years,' Skinny had predicted. 'Ten years hard time.'

Skinny, I thought, recalling the way he had looked at me when he had put me out of his car, as if daring me to defy him, and remembering, too, the watery red froth that had formed at one corner of his mouth as he had eaten his ketchup-covered breakfast.

Now that I had them I would give Skinny the slides I had in my pocket, Stacey's illegible books, the pages of meaningless jumble she had given to Ellis, knowing he did not read them; and I would allow DeLloyd to go ahead with the deal—I would even provide the cash—certain that there was no established link back to the agency. I would make it appear that DeLloyd had been acting on his own all along.

I closed my hand around my keys and squeezed tightly, feeling the sharp ridges dig into my palm.

Skinny wanted someone; I would give him DeLloyd.

I loosened my grip, held up my keys, and shook them before I had time to think too much about what I was doing.

'You don't need to see either Stacey or

Ellis,' I said. 'I can get in the box.'

For a long, thoughtful moment DeLloyd did not move, then very slowly he turned away from the window. Back-lit, with the daylight behind him, his dark features were difficult to see, his expression hard to read.

'Ain't that handy?' he said.

I felt his gaze on me, his dark, looming presence.

'I looking out the window, I think: I where he was last night—if I him and those bullets come by—it would of run me off. Most likely I still be running, trying to hide.' DeLloyd paused. When he spoke again his voice suddenly lost its vowelly slur; it became much crisper, sharper, with more of an edge. 'You wouldn't try to fuck with me, would you, my friend?'

CHAPTER THIRTEEN

The bank's ceiling was high and vaulted, stately, and the finish materials—glass, stone, hard dark wood—were solid and cool to the touch, expensive and enduring. The air was dehumidified, cool and crisp. My leather heels made a distinct, important sound on the polished marbled floor.

I was very familiar with the bank—when I was deciding where my office should be, I had, in fact, chosen to locate near it because it was the only bank in New Orleans that dealt directly with the banks in Central America. So after DeLloyd dropped me off in front of it I knew exactly how to get to the safe deposit vault, which was across the lobby, up the steps, and down a short hall. I knew many of the bank's tellers and officers, the conservatively dressed men and women who now either stared silently at me as I passed or pretended not to notice me as they shuffled papers busily or dug with sudden interest through their files or desk drawers—but the questions were there in their eyes, in their furtive glances, and in the rebuking hush that seemed to follow me. I knew where to sign in, where I should wait, when to produce my key. In the vault, the neat rows of stainless steel boxes reminded me, as they always did, of the neat rows of crypts in a mausoleum.

Across from the vault were small rooms, little more than booths with a counter, a chair, an ashtray; and I took the box to the room on the end, the only room with a window. Twenty feet below me the midday traffic was heavy. Cars waited patiently in line as delivery boys on bicycles wove in and out between them. On the sidewalk, just as I remembered, were men in suits and women in bright dresses on their way either to or from lunch.

The large safe deposit box was very nearly

empty, containing only a few papers and one thick sheaf of bills. I emptied it methodically, placing the papers on one side and the cash on the other before I put the box on the floor. Among the papers there were only the titles to the agency's lot and building and to my father's car, a lapsed insurance policy, and, strangely, I thought, the Honduran birth certificates for my sister and me. The two certificates were elaborately sealed, ribboned, signed, and imprinted with our tiny footprints, no larger than the heel of my hand. I set them on top of the other papers, and as I thumbed through the thick sheaf of bills, counting them, now and again I looked at our footprints, regarding them curiously, amused to note that my sister had been born with feet much larger than mine.

The cash totaled just over seven thousand dollars, not an unsubstantial amount but hardly as much as DeLloyd had believed I'd find—hardly as much as the hundred eighty-five thousand dollars he had said he needed to complete the deal. I divided the money into three equal piles, bound the piles tightly with rubber bands, put each one in a different pocket in my jacket. I hooked one leg over the arm of the chair and looked out at the street, wondering what I should do, feeling very secure in that small, locked, soundproof room and reluctant to leave it, reluctant to meet again with that rebuking hush that seemed to follow me. Suddenly I felt very tired and sleepy; I took a deep breath, rose to my feet, returned the papers to the box, and closed it.

* * *

I said to the woman behind the desk, 'I'd like to find out who's been into my safe deposit box.'

The woman was filling out a form, writing in the small, rectangular spaces provided, and she replied without looking up, 'Your name and box number.'

I told her my name and put my key on her desk.

She glanced at the number on the key, rolled her chair backward, and consulted a small, tattered file; after a moment she removed a card, rolled her chair back, handed me the card and my key, and continued to work on her form.

I read the card, tapped it against my thumb, read it again: Stacey Veldran had been into the box the last four workdays in a row.

I thought about Stacey and, sadly, about what Ellis had told me about her. I knew now I was only a half-step behind her, and I was not certain I wanted to catch up.

* * *

The bank's international department was four floors above the lobby. Located in a large, windowless room, the space was brightly lit and was divided up only by heavy equipment and furniture: high-powered computers, oversized two-person desks, and a wall-sized display board that flashed in two-inch-high numbers the constantly changing values of international currency. The walls and ceilings were painted white; the floor was covered with a soft dark gray material, cushioned and static-free. Behind the constant roaring hum of the air-conditioning and the machines, there was a charged vitality in that large room, a frenetic energy I had always liked, a feeling that each moment was important. Because the room was kept very cold, most of the women wore sweaters; none of the men removed their coats.

I was looking for my neighbor, Marge, hoping to catch her before she left for the day. While Marge was supposed to go to work at four in the morning and to get off at one in the afternoon, she often ran late and the bank allowed her to add the minutes she had missed early to the end of her day. It worked well for both of them, she had told me, I at my bedroom window, loosening my tie, glancing through my mail, she on her roof terrace, fussing with the bushy plants that lined her parapet. That way, she had explained, she got to sleep through an extra snooze-alarm before she had to get up, and the bank got its full eight hours. Most of our conversations had been like that, very brief, rather transient, neighborly in an urban sort of way—and it made me glad I had helped her to get her apartment. Once or twice I had seen her here at the bank, but for business she had referred me to an officer.

I glanced at my watch. It was after one o'clock. If Marge had been on time that morning I had missed her; but just as I was about to ask for her I saw her, leaning toward a computer screen in much the same posture she leaned toward her plants when she was watering them—curious, a bit concerned, patient, and determined.

I moved toward her desk in as straight a line as possible, going around the desks, chairs, and computers, pushing aside wheeled carts that held downward-hanging files, stepping over the heavy black cables that crisscrossed the floor. I stood right beside her before she noticed me; she looked up with a start.

Her eyes momentarily went wide, then her face relaxed, and she said merrily, 'Mr. Tony Curbel. What a surprise to see *you* here.' She followed her bright greeting with a wink and smiled a perky smile.

I hesitated a moment, uncertain how to ask the favor I wanted of her, and she added,

'Commodities prices are upstairs, sir. Soy beans and grain are on the fifth floor.' She smiled again. 'Marijuana is a little higher.'

I did not think I had heard her correctly, and I just looked at her, my eyes narrowing.

Marge pushed herself away from her desk, draped one arm over the back of her chair, and said with feigned exasperation, 'That was a joke, Tony,' and rolled her eyes heavenward as she shook her head.

I smiled tentatively at first, then I felt my smile grow broader because with that first joke about it I realized I had truly started back, out of jail.

I said, 'I have a favor to ask.' I paused. 'And it's smokeless.'

Marge laughed at that, a good-natured jovial laugh, then her bright sharp eyes took on a serious cast. 'What's up?' she asked.

I hesitated again because I knew what I was about to ask could very well get her fired: I knew my favor would violate the bank's ethics and, though I wasn't certain, possibly even federal law.

I said, 'I need to trace some funds transfers.'

Marge had read my hesitation. It showed in her eyes, in her sudden misgiving: she knew the money I needed to trace was not my own. With both hands she reached up to the sweater that was draped across her shoulders and threw it back, over the back of her chair, then she looked to see that it had not fallen to the floor, glancing around quickly as she did so.

'The transfers were made by one of your employees, right?' she said, looking back at me.

It was not a question, it was the out she needed to cover herself, and I chided myself for not thinking of it first.

'Right,' I replied. 'The transfers were made by one of my employees.'

Marge sat up straight, moved her chair near her desk, placed her fingers over the computer keyboard, poised. She touched a few buttons, and the computer screen cleared.

'Who received the money?' she asked, her tone no longer jovial but curt and businesslike.

'That's what I don't know,' I replied.

Marge looked at me out of the corners of her eyes, a quick, hard look that flicked past.

'The transfers would have been made within the last several months—the easiest one to find probably took place within the last four days.'

I was playing a hunch, assuming that, if Stacey had taken the agency's money, she would not have kept it around.

'Directly from an account?' Marge asked.

I shook my head regretfully.

'No,' I replied. 'It would have been

cash—or a cashier's check.'

Marge shot me that same quick look, but it was even harder this time, edged with disapproval: to transfer cash rather than to transfer from a standing account was, at best, suspicious.

'You're not giving me much to go on,' she said, turning her head enough to look directly at me. 'Your employee could have used another name or even a company name.'

'I know,' I said absently, trying to think, trying to recall any other information I had that might narrow down the search.

'Let's start with the name,' Marge suggested.

'Veldran,' I said, and spelled it out. 'Stacey Veldran.'

Marge glanced around again before she typed in an access code, Stacey's name, another code. She drummed her fingers on the table, then rested her chin on her hand as she waited for the computer to respond to the commands that she had given it.

'*Nada*,' she said after a few seconds, shaking her head, then, as if she needed to translate, she added, 'Nothing.'

I rubbed my hands together, palms flat, in small irregular circles.

Nada, I thought, that one word of Spanish seeming somehow important, making me feel I was onto something. *Nada*, I thought again, allowing the word to roll around in my head.

I tucked my lower lip between my teeth and bit down on it, feeling the stiff soreness in my jaw more than the pain in my lip, recalling the last Spanish I had spoken. That morning I had said to Señor Esperoza, '*Le regresaré sus hijos*' (I will get you back your sons), to which he had replied, '*Su padre está bien*' (Your father is well).

Señor Esperoza, I thought, troubled because I knew then how it all fit together.

For years, Stacey had told me, my father had been taking the agency's money to Panama, hiding its source behind the extraordinarily stringent Panamanian bank secrecy laws. If that was so, then, precisely because Esperoza wanted to change those laws, he was someone my father would have tried to cultivate, someone he would have tried to make a friend so that he would learn firsthand what progress he was making. My father would have used Esperoza's bank, and he would have introduced him to both Ellis and Stacey, trying to gain his trust. So naturally Señor Esperoza would have been likely to go to my father when *he* needed a favor, when he needed his sons gotten out of Panama—just as Stacey would have gone to Señor Esperoza when she needed to arrange the secret transfer of money because likely, too, he was the only Panamanian banker she knew. And with her transfer arrangements in place and the Tees-and-Blues deal in progress, it must have seemed too good to be true when Esperoza came to them, needing a favor that, if used correctly, would provide diversion on both ends, in both New Orleans and Panama City, a diversion that would turn them all against each other, giving her time to put the money together, take it, and transfer it to her own account, out of the country.

I felt Marge looking at me questioningly, and I said almost reluctantly, 'The money might have gone to the Banco de Santander, Panama City,' knowing that if the money *had* been transferred there I was right on all counts.

The keyboard keys clicked as Marge quickly gave the computer the name of the bank, and I felt myself hoping against my own solid reasoning, clinging to the slim possibility that, since there was no record of Stacey's name in the computer, I was wrong.

I heard Marge say, 'Got it,' softly, more to herself than to me, and I saw the computer screen fill with information, showing the amount of the transfer, the name of the person who had made it, the form of payment.

Marge whistled softly and tapped her finger against the screen.

'Wow, Tony,' she said, 'if that's how much your *employees* make, you're rich as sin.' She smiled briefly, then studied the display, her round face curious. After a moment she nodded to herself and sat back. 'That's why the computer didn't find anything at first,' she said, gesturing toward the display before she pressed one key three times, clearing the screen. 'The name-of-record wasn't exactly the same one we gave it.'

'Right,' I said, acknowledging her explanation, reading again the name-of-record, watching as the luminous yellow-green letters faded from the screen. For a very brief moment the letters left behind dark imprints of themselves on the inside of the glass, disturbing brown-black shadows that read, Stacey Veldran Curbelo.

CHAPTER FOURTEEN

I did not understand why Stacey had gone into the agency's safe deposit box four workdays in a row, the last two of them—the previous two days—*after* she had sent all but a small amount of the agency's cash to her own account in the Banco de Santander. The more I thought about it, the more convinced I became that I must have overlooked something in the box, something that would explain her repeated visits; so after I rode the elevator down to the first floor I went back up to the safe deposit vault, crossing the lobby by the same route I had taken a half hour before, then going back up the steps and back down the short hall.

The woman at the desk was completing another lengthy form, and she gave me a very cool look when I asked to get in the box again, pointedly looking at her watch—making it very clear that the bank's closing time was only a half hour away—before she told me that the box was already checked out.

I thought about that for only a moment, not really surprised to learn that Stacey was back for a fifth consecutive day; I glanced along the row of doors to the small rooms across from the vault. Only one door was closed, the door to the room on the end—the room I had used myself—and I went directly to it and pushed it open, before the woman behind the desk could protest, before Stacey could do more than glance up from the chair where she was sitting, her expression a mix of surprise and annoyance, the safe deposit box there on the counter beside her, beside her purse, still closed.

'Miss *Curbelo*,' I said, using the name she had assumed as a terse greeting, putting an edge on the words.

I stepped inside the small room, closed the door, and leaned back against it.

Stacey looked at me briefly, then turned her head, looking first at the wall above the counter, then turning her head farther, looking out the window, out at the gray granite face of the building across the street.

I looked at her, looking out, almost feeling her agitation as she mulled over the greeting I had used, putting it together with my sudden appearance; and I allowed her time to figure out that I knew both about the money she had taken and about what she had done with it before I asked, 'Why?' quietly, that one word hanging, heavy in the air, placing the burden of silence on her.

When finally she turned back, I heard her blouse rustle, still stiff with starch, and the slow swish her linen slacks made sliding on the chair.

'I hated him,' she said evenly. 'I hated Ellis for what he did to my mother and me—I suppose you know about that, too?' She glanced at me briefly, then looked away.

I did not reply to her but thought about what Ellis had told me that morning, about how, during his convalescence in Mochita, in the late afternoons he had taken the rowboat and floated downstream, to the bend in the river, where his nurse, Stacey's mother, had met him on the gravel bar, there with tortillas and beer. I thought about how something so seemingly harmless and pleasant had gotten all twisted around, made sordid and destructive.

'My mother and father had been childless for three years,' Stacey went on, 'when she went to work for the Curbelos. Two months later, she was pregnant. They all knew what had happened—everyone knew. In Mochita I'm still called *la bastarda*, the bastard girl.' In one quick motion Stacey took a single cigarette from her purse and lit it, exhaling the smoke at the wall. 'My mother was seventeen years old when I was born.'

Seventeen years old, I thought, thinking involuntarily of Randy, my seventeen-year-old cellmate, catching an image of him sitting on the corner of the metal-frame bunk, hunched over, his thin shoulders rounded, as he dipped the needle into the ink, again and again, bringing it out, studying the drops that formed on its tip; then very quickly I shifted my thoughts back to the present, before I could speculate about what sort of night he had spent.

'Did you suggest the "float"?' I asked. 'The loans?'

Stacey reached for the ashtray the bank provided and pulled it along the counter, sliding it.

'It seemed like a good idea at the time,' she replied. 'Ellis and Carl just left the money in here'—she motioned toward the safe deposit box—'sometimes for months on end. It seemed such a waste.'

When she glanced up, her eyes surprised me: they were softer than I had expected, more uncertain than angry or evasive.

'So you began to use it? You and

DeLloyd?'

Stacey took a pull on her cigarette, flicked an ash into the ashtray.

'Not the way you think,' she said. 'Not at first—my first investment was in high-yield bonds.' She smiled to herself, thinly, a vaguely amused smile. 'I made five thousand dollars and thought I was ready for Wall Street.' For a long moment she looked blankly at the ashtray, then her smile faded and her eyes came back to me, cooler now, more composed. 'It wasn't until much later that Ellis told me to let DeLloyd use the money, too.'

'Ellis told you to let DeLloyd use the money?' It was a question the way I said it, doubtfully.

Stacey's dark eyes held mine.

'Ellis didn't hire DeLloyd away from the garage to help with the collections, Tony.' Her eyes took on a faintly condescending cast, as if she were speaking to a child. 'Of course he wanted DeLloyd to use the money: he wanted him to work his deals.'

I started to add, 'Or *you* wanted him to work his deals,' but I thought better of questioning her so blatantly when she seemed so willing to talk. I brought my hand to my jaw and rubbed it, prodding the soreness, hoping the pain would make me more alert, wondering why, although what she had said made sense, it did not seem to fit.

I knew Ellis. I knew his natural gregariousness, how easily he got to know people, talking to strangers he met as if he had known them for years. And while certainly he would not hesitate to use those around him if the need arose, he would not set out to recruit someone with a particular purpose in mind—that was something my father would do. So it seemed more likely to me that Ellis had hired DeLloyd just as DeLloyd had said, to make the collections, and Stacey, not Ellis, had put him up to the deals, telling him that she could provide the cash if he could make the connections. Later on, when Ellis or my father had found out about it—or perhaps Stacey had simply told them—they had let it continue, wanting so badly the extra money that would allow them to buy Mochita out of debt that they had overlooked their own vulnerability, the power that that acquiescence had given Stacey over them.

'I see,' I said out loud, and I meant it: once Stacey had begun to act in their stead, illegally, the trouble had begun.

Stacey said, 'You'd think they would have learned from their first mistake.'

I moved my hand forward from my jaw and placed one finger across my lips, thinking: she had seen the opportunity to hurt Ellis, and she had taken it.

'What mistake was that?' I asked absently,

wondering what her next ploy would be.

Stacey took another pull on her cigarette and exhaled the smoke through her nose.

'The mistake that got you sent to jail, Tony: when the customs people seized their thousand-pound shipment of marijuana.'

Even before I could replay to myself what she had said I felt a flush rise to my cheeks. A deep hollow coldness came into my chest. In the window I saw a flash of movement, a very faint reflection of myself, features blurred, stepped forward aggressively, angrily. In Stacey I saw the quick, recoiling fear, the cowering I had seen in her when I had met her in jail, but now I was not puzzled by that fear because it seemed only appropriate, the proper response: I, too, would recoil from the anger of the man I had willfully sent to jail. With both hands I reached out and grabbed the front of her blouse, bunching the starched cotton in my fists as I lifted her out of her chair and pushed her back, pressing her against the single sheet of glass in the window, feeling it flex.

'Do you know what you did?' I said, shaking her, my voice breaking. 'Do you have any idea what jail is like?'

I shook her again, harder, knowing then exactly what had happened, how Stacey had been trying to hurt Ellis when she began to deal dope, thinking she could destroy him by setting up a deal so that it appeared he was responsible, then informing on him herself. And it had almost worked. Almost. What she had not counted on was the way my father would handle it, forcing me at the risk of my entire family not to defend myself, to accept the blame. But with me out of the way she had only to wait, covering herself—and now she was trying again, setting up another deal and making it go bad.

I pushed her back harder against the glass.

'Do you have any idea what you are doing? You're putting us all at risk. All of us.'

Stacey just looked at me, wide-eyed at first, then very coldly as the fear left her face.

I threw my hands away from her in a gesture of contempt, as if I could not stand even to touch her. A button popped from her blouse.

I turned away, roughly throwing the chair out of my way, seeing the gray steel safe deposit box on the counter and starting to throw it, too, but picking it up instead, opening it, knowing instinctively what had brought her back to the vault on consecutive days.

'This is mine,' I said harshly, reaching into the safe deposit box and taking out my birth certificate, waving it at her. 'Mine. Do you understand that? You will never be a Curbelo. Never. No matter what you do. No matter how many bank accounts you open. No matter how much you dream about it.

You will never be a Curbelo.'

With disgust I threw the certificate at her. It caught the air and floated before it dropped between us, pulled down on the bottom edge by the weight of its seal.

Stacey watched the certificate drop, her jaw slack, a stunned, almost horrified look on her face; then she forced her eyes away and after a moment began to smooth her blouse nervously, impatiently, using her fingertips to press down the wrinkles my fists had made. She glanced around uncertainly, picked up her purse, prepared to leave. But I stayed where I was, between the door and her, unmoving, the anger still in me.

'Let me leave,' she ordered tersely, and tried to push past me.

I grabbed her upper arm and gripped it tightly, just holding it, holding her back, not through with her yet.

She tried to pull free and when she could not she came at me, pushing against my chest in short, hard, furious shoves that rocked me back until I bumped against the door, blocking it completely; but still she kept on, beating the heels of her hands against me until with one final push she stepped back, looking up at me, her eyes hate-filled and fiery.

'Yes,' she hissed, 'I know exactly what I've done. I've hurt you, all of you. And there is nothing you can do about it. Not one thing.

I've hurt all you fine, respectable Curbelos. I've made you pay for what you did to me.' She tossed her head in a gesture of angry defiance. Her voice was derisive, cutting. 'You're helpless, Tony. You understand that, don't you? Being helpless? Isn't that what being in jail is all about, having to stay there and take whatever comes along? Whether or not you did anything to deserve it, you're forced to stay there, waiting?'

The force of her bitter, restrained fury hit me in a way that made my own anger seem insignificant in comparison. I stood very still as she went on, watching her closely, understanding what I had only sensed in her before, seeing her cool façade crack and the corrosive hatred, the bitterness, the contempt that ran just behind it, just beneath the surface.

'*I* waited. I waited for years, lifetimes to a little girl, looking out at my father's plantation and his big white house, wondering why he didn't come for me, knowing he could, he *had to* get me away from the horror he had created.'

Stacey tossed her head again, and a glass-hard glint appeared in her eyes.

'My mother's husband wouldn't call me by my name, Tony. From the time I was born he called me *la bastarda*—that's the name I grew up with. He worked on the Curbelo plantation as a *cañero*, a cane-cutter, and he hated it. He hated the Curbelos for their money and their power—they all did, everyone who worked there. But he had *me*, his own half-Curbelo *bastarda* to blame. Every day I'd have to stand there as he told me how my father had taken him away from his crew to clean out the stable or how my uncle had doubled up his work. Every day there was something, some new complaint. And if I tried to protest that it wasn't my fault, I wasn't a Curbelo—if I even looked him in the face—he'd slap me for my *insolence*, for being just like *them*; so I looked down, watching his filthy, dust-covered feet, praying he wouldn't start to drink because when he drank, believe me, it got a whole lot worse, and all that time, for years, *for years*, I could only think, he will come for me soon. My father will come for me.'

Stacey stared at me, hard, and I glanced away, looking over her shoulder, out the window, seeing the well-dressed people walking past on the sidewalk below, recalling how Stacey had told me almost as soon as I had met her that what she remembered most about her mother's husband was his feet, how gray dust had coated them and how it had cracked near his toes, like skin.

'And when Ellis did finally come to get me, what? Did he ever, even once, admit that I'm his daughter? Did he give me his name? Better yet, Tony, what did his family do?

Those fine, upright Curbelos? Did they invite me into their home? Did they acknowledge me in any way at all?' Angrily she waved one hand at the floor, at my birth certificate there where it had dropped, face up, its gold seal shining dully. 'And you think you have to tell *me* I will never be a Curbelo? I have *not* been a Curbelo my whole life.'

There was nothing I could say. I knew what she had related very likely was true. I pursed my lips and allowed my eyes to wander before I glanced back at her, cautiously, almost furtively; but she was waiting for that, waiting with her eyes steady on mine.

'Until recently,' she said, derision mixing with her anger, 'when your two uncles in Mochita began to sell out. Then I was supposed to forget everything that had come before. I was supposed to summon up all my good Curbelo-family loyalty and work even harder, make even more money to save the land where I've never been welcome and the big white house where I've never been invited. Isn't that right, Tony? Isn't that what I was supposed to do?'

She glared at me, not expecting a reply, and I could see that she was about to go on.

I said, 'I don't know what you were supposed to do, Stacey,' surprising her, breaking her momentum. 'I only know what you did.'

Behind her hard anger a questioning look came into her eyes, a mild, triumphant curiosity.

'Somehow you convinced DeLloyd that you needed a deal, a big one. You probably said that you needed it for Ellis—to save him, of course, not to destroy him. When DeLloyd told you about Lips and his Tees-and-Blues, you went for it. But Lips didn't. Maybe he suspected something. Maybe he just didn't want to deal with you. You're a woman, and you're Hispanic. You had two strikes against you before you even got into his game.'

I shrugged, waiting to see if Stacey would add something to—or deny—any part of my speculation; but she didn't.

I shrugged again before I went on, 'But you wanted that deal. You wanted it so badly you put pressure on Lips by setting him up on a false rape charge. Lips saw you were serious and decided to put the deal in motion. You made the deposit from here'—I tapped one knuckle against the safe deposit box—'and the Tees came in. Along about that time Señor Esperoza appeared, needing his sons smuggled out of Panama. It was perfect, almost too good to be true. All you had to do was to put his sons where they wouldn't be found, and you had the diversion you needed. While everyone was out trying to find the two boys, you got ready to close the deal, and you transferred your getaway money out of the country—enough money both to destroy the agency when it was lost and enough for you to live comfortably for quite a while.' I tapped the safe deposit box again, a thought suddenly occurring to me. 'The cash you left in here was just to show a criminal intent to close the deal. It was just to satisfy the district attorney that there was, in fact, a conspiracy to distribute a controlled dangerous substance. The deal itself is a setup. It's not supposed to go through: it's supposed to get Ellis and Carl sent to jail. And that's where it is right now, Stacey. That's where you are'—I gestured around the small room—'coming here every day, trying to convince yourself to go ahead with it because you know if you do you really have cut it.' I shook my head slowly from side to side. 'If you go through with it you get your revenge but you lose the closest thing to family that you have.'

'My mother is my family,' Stacey snapped, the brittle edge on her voice changed just slightly, tinged with defensiveness.

I shook my head again, trying to feel more for her than I did, knowing possibly that I *would* feel for her if my own anger was not still there, restrained now, but there in an ice-cold fury when I considered what she was trying to do and what she had done, the year I had spent in jail.

'Where are the two boys?' I asked. 'Esperoza's sons?'

Stacey did not reply to me but turned away to face the window, looking out. She wrapped one hand, the hand that held her purse, across her middle and brought the other hand to her face. Just then I felt certain she was thinking of Ellis, and I tried to play on those thoughts, nudging them along.

I said quietly, 'In his own way, Stacey, Ellis is pretty sharp. Not much gets past him—not much about people, anyway. Likely you already know that, how he is.'

Stacey did not move at all, but I could tell that she was listening. It was in the way she held herself, tense and noticeably still.

'I think he knows what you're up to. Maybe he doesn't know the details—maybe he doesn't know about your deal with Lips or about the money you've transferred—but he knows you're trying to hurt him. He'd have read that in *you*. But even so, he couldn't bring himself to stop you. That's why he made you get me out of jail, isn't it? To have someone fight for him—and so indirectly you'd have to know that he knew. What does that tell you, Stacey, that he couldn't bring himself to stop you?'

Stacey dropped her hands, stood erect, put one hand in the pocket of her slacks. For a moment she seemed about to say something; but when she did not, I went on.

'I don't think you meant it to go this far, really. I think you expected to be stopped, if not by Ellis, then by the events themselves. Who would ever have guessed that Lips would actually come through or that Señor Esperoza would show up when he did? It's almost as if the circumstances conspired to keep you going, never giving you the chance to be caught so that you could confront Ellis and tell him what you just told me, show him your anger before any real damage had been done.'

Stacey rolled one shoulder forward and back, a gesture of acknowledgment or a gesture of indifference, it was hard to tell which.

'There's only one thing that you've figured wrongly, Stacey, one basic mistake that you've made.' I paused because I knew what I was about to say was a risk, the kind of speculation that could very well work against me.

There was a sharp, insistent knock at the door.

'Just a moment,' I said over my shoulder, tersely; then to Stacey, 'Throughout all this you've misdirected your anger—just like your mother's husband misdirected his.'

I saw her stiffen, a quick tension shoot through her in a way that showed I was on to something she had considered herself.

'You've blamed Ellis for what that man did to you just as he blamed the Curbelos—including you—for his own unhappiness.'

The knock was repeated, and, annoyed, I turned and opened the door, seeing just outside it the woman I had seen twice before at her desk, filling out forms.

'It is two o'clock,' the woman announced, tapping her finger on her oversize watch, her face screwed up in a sour scowl. 'The bank is now closed.'

I started simply to shut the door on her, but before I could, Stacey squeezed past on my left, slipping around me neatly and out, walking away quickly, not looking back. For a long moment I just stared after her, watching her go down the short hall and down the steps to the lobby.

'Damn,' I swore under my breath, softly but emphatically, just loud enough that the sour-faced woman would hear.

'The bank is closed,' she repeated, and turned away huffily, going back to her desk.

Briefly I leaned against the doorframe before I turned around myself, knowing I had to return the box to the vault. Reflexly, I patted my pockets, feeling for my keys, found them, and bent over to pick up my birth certificate, noticing as I did so that the certificate was creased now, smudged on its seal, stepped on, I supposed, by Stacey in her haste to leave.

CHAPTER FIFTEEN

It was well past lunchtime, and out on the street the pedestrian traffic had thinned, the food-minded crush reduced to a business-as-usual throng. Deliverymen and secretaries on errands had largely replaced the coat-and-tie crowd, the businessmen, lawyers, and accountants who now were behind the windows overhead, behind their desks, weighing, judging, and figuring secure in their work. It was hard for me not to feel some envy of them, a painful awareness of what I had lost, but it felt good to be back on the street and I allowed myself to enjoy it, stopping for a sandwich and a cold bottle of beer, idly shopping the store-front windows, comparing the actual feel of downtown to the memories of it I had had while in jail.

Nothing significant had changed. A few small stores had new owners or were closed. A large old building had been torn down, a new large building put up in its place. A few small trees had been planted. Across Canal Street—the wide boulevard that was the boundary between the business district and the French Quarter— I saw my old newsdealer, still there on his corner, hawking his papers, his baseball cap askew, so I crossed over, and as I approached he gave me his familiar wink. I smiled in return, pleased to be remembered, asked for a local paper and waited, as usual, glancing at the headlines as he dug in his apron for change. At that moment I felt a peculiar satisfaction, a deep sense that all would be right again, that changed so unexpectedly, so quickly, it made a flat spot, an almost vacuumlike stillness inside me. Looking at the newsdealer's hand when he extended it, offering my change, seeing the silver coins on his callused, newsprint-stained palm, for a fraction of a second that moment and my memory of other moments just like it seemed to run together, blurring, so indistinguishable one from the other I could not tell for certain where I was, there on the corner with the coins in front of me—or there in jail, remembering it.

I took the coins, nodded once, turned away, and it was several steps before I came back to myself, knowing again with certainty both where I was and what I was doing.

I stopped on the curb and pretended to scan the paper, giving myself time to think; but before I could even find some likely reason for that disquieting confusion I felt the hair on the back of my neck bristle. I looked around, right and left, feeling Skinny's undeniable presence, hearing him say in his rude, nasal twang, 'You can be back in the joint, Curbel,' and snapping his fingers. 'Just like that.'

But no one was even near me.

A chill ran up my spine.

Just like that, I thought, reading very easily the message I had given myself, now very clear of any confusion.

I stepped off the curb and started home, to my apartment, avoiding the route that I usually took.

* * *

The apartment was cool, almost cold, the air-conditioning still set very low, forgotten when I had left before, leaving with DeLloyd, leaving Esperoza's two men in my tub. I adjusted the thermostat and went into the bedroom, then the bathroom, knowing the apartment was empty but checking it just the same, noting the deep dent in the side of the tub, the towels and the neckties on the floor, one small drop of blood on the wall.

In the bedroom I threw the pillows to one end of the bed and pulled the quilt flat before I emptied my pockets, taking out the assortment of things I had collected in the twenty-four hours just past: the piece of paper on which DeLloyd had written reluctantly; the room key from the motel near the airport; the gun in its odd, walletlike case; the slides, Stacey's books, and the cash she had left behind. Seeing them like that, laid out side by side, it was hard not to review the day I had had—and easy to know what I had to do.

In the bathroom I found a scissors; I moved a chair near the bed and sat forward, hunched over, elbows on knees as I read the paper, then cut each page into strips. When I had finished with the first section I took the strips and cut them again, crossways, putting each piece on top of a sheaf of bills, checking its size, aligning it, making sure that when I put the thin paper between the bills the edges would not be revealed.

I had to assume that Stacey would remain fixed in her intention, that she still had hope of destroying the agency and would allow the deal to go forward; and no matter what, I knew *I* could not be the one to prevent it from taking place. I could not allow it in any way to appear that I had warned DeLloyd off: if I did, then Skinny would know—Lips would be sure to tell him—and I would be back in jail that night, leaving Stacey free to try again, differently, more cleverly, until finally she came up with a way to get the revenge that she wanted. So I had to pad out the money; I had to make it seem there was much more than there actually was, enough, at least, to make a payment—enough to show a criminal intent.

I began on the second section of the paper, reading the local news, the small events of the city, and cutting those pages up as I mapped out my own intentions.

I knew that Stacey had to have a second set of books—and perhaps even a third. She would have needed one to show Ellis, one for herself, and perhaps yet another for Skinny; and while the set I had was the illegible one, the set she had made for show, I knew I could make it work to exonerate Ellis: I could repeat her explanation, display her handwriting, verify the few dates and amounts I could decipher. And because she had taken the money itself and transferred it out of the country—the bank's records were quite clear about that—it would be easy to show that the deal had been financed with money that Ellis had never received.

I saw a short article about the city's budget, and I read it, dismayed to learn that the jail's money had been cut.

Yet there *was* a deal—there was a buyer and a seller; a deposit had been made—and someone had to have arranged it. Someone had to have initiated the conspiracy that Skinny intended to stop. And with Stacey working as Skinny's informant all along, by elimination that left DeLloyd.

DeLloyd, I thought, recalling immediately the size of him, wondering when he would come for the money.

DeLloyd knew Lips, and he had made the initial approach. DeLloyd, too, had had access to the collections. The way I would tell it to Skinny, he had acted alone when he had held back the money to make the deposit, and when the deal had been set, he had planned to use the agency's money to complete the exchange—I had seen him myself, in Stacey's house, searching for her key. Later I had brought him what money there was, the money that Skinny himself would find on him when he made his arrest.

DeLloyd.

It was all DeLloyd—or so I would make it appear.

And best of all, I thought, a bitter taste in my throat, *DeLloyd is unlikely to implicate Ellis, his friend, the man who got him away from parking cars and taught him to read and to write.*

Carefully I placed the first few pieces I had clipped, padding out a thin sheaf of bills, making it appear very thick.

God help me, I thought, *when he makes bail and puts it all together.*

* * *

When my doorbell rang I was ready for it, up out of the chair where I had been waiting and moving even before the button had been released. I pressed the buzzer, opened the door, and waited; when I heard no one on the steps, I buzzed again, then listened through the intercom, hearing DeLloyd over the noise of the stop-and-go traffic behind him.

'No use buzzin',' he said, his voice returned to its vowelly slur, not at all like the sharp tone he had used with me before. 'You comin' down.'

'What about the money?' I asked, keeping my voice low, hesitant.

'You bring it with you,' he replied. 'I double-parked. I make the block, you be out in front.' It was not a request the way he said it, tersely, impatiently.

I pressed the buzzer twice, making it click, ending the exchange and showing that I agreed.

I had not expected to leave the apartment and I did not have on my coat; so I went to get it, looking around for my keys as I did so, quickly changing shoes, taking the brown paper bag with the money from behind the pillows where I had left it. It was a small bag, but the padded sheaves of bills gave a good weight to it, a solid feel. I rolled up the top and gripped it tightly as I left, starting to turn off the lights but leaving them on instead, hoping I would be back in just a few minutes.

This is better, I thought as I went down the stairs. *It will go better in the car*. But I knew the thought was without foundation: either he would count the money, or he would not. That depended on my luck. I took the steps two at a time, too fast, feeling my heart begin to thump. On the second-floor landing, I made myself stop, then go on more slowly.

Outside, it was raining lightly, a steady, annoying drizzle. I stayed under the balcony, out of the rain, and waited. When DeLloyd did not appear in a minute or two I began to pace, walking back and forth on the dry strip of sidewalk that ran the length of the building. Only when the streetlights came on, flickering hesitantly before getting fully lit, did I really notice that it was dusk, a full five hours since I had left the bank.

Hurry up and wait, I thought, trying to relax, forcing myself to smile inside. *This I can do in jail.*

And I did smile, thinly, because I had said that same thing to myself earlier, when I had been dawdling away the afternoon, straightening up my apartment, dozing in a chair, appreciating the quiet and the stillness—all small things I enjoyed that, of course, I had not been able to do in jail. But then as now, the waiting disturbed me. Nagging doubts crept into the stillness: I was worried that DeLloyd would discover my ruse, and even if it worked, I was worried that Skinny would not believe me. I hardly needed to remind myself that Skinny was very clever and very quick—and likely to have information that I did not. But even as I constructed different scenarios, asking myself, 'What if . . . ?' and trying to anticipate what might go wrong, I realized I was in a way deluding myself, hiding in the immediate, questioning only the events because I did not want to question myself: I did not want to see too clearly what sort of person it appeared I was becoming. And that realization made it hard not to try to go behind the events and onto the shakier ground of the motivations that had formed them.

Now as earlier, I missed my wife. I wondered what she would have said, what she would have advised me to do.

'Does the end justify these rather radical means?' she would likely have asked.

And that was a tough one. I thought so, but I was not certain. I was giving up one person to save several others—on the face of it a tenable explanation—but I wondered how much of my reasoning was simply self-serving justification, a way both to save Mochita and to keep myself out of jail.

'And if you do lose Mochita, what will happen? Jail you can survive.'

That was tougher still. If I lost the land I lost what little stability there was in my life. If I lost the land I lost my connection to my family and my heritage and with it would go my confidence and my self-respect—I would lose what little I had of my mother and my wife.

'You will do what you have to do,' my father had said, and only now, waiting on that darkening street, did I seem to understand him. How much harder it must have been for him, to decide to give me, his own son, up to jail. What had he thought in his worst moments, at night, tired, alone in his big house? What had he felt when he had read my angry, bitter letters?

I did not know. I did not know whether or not I was right. I did not know why I had assumed an obligation I had never wanted or how I would feel later, when DeLloyd was in jail and I tried to explain it to myself. But I did know the devastating loss I would feel if I could not go to stand on the land at all, if only to curse it for the price it had extracted.

Up the street DeLloyd's German car came into view, dark and low-slung, throwing spray as it moved very fast.

'*Yo soy Curbelo*,' I said out loud, softly, holding the brown paper bag tightly, stepping down off the curb. 'I am a Curbel.'

DeLloyd stopped just in front of me, then reached across and threw open the passenger-side door.

The car's metal gleamed; droplets had formed on the roof and the hood.

I leaned down to hand him the brown paper bag, extending one arm out in front of me.

'Get in,' he ordered roughly, ignoring the bag.

I did not ask why but did as he said, hardly

in the seat before he accelerated and jerked the wheel, sliding in front of one car and up past another, passing on the right.

'You got the money?' he asked, not looking at me.

'Every penny,' I replied, neglecting to add, 'Every penny there was,' an amount far short of what he expected. 'What do you want me to do with it?'

DeLloyd braked, then accelerated again, jerking the wheel, spinning it, slipping between a car and a lamppost so closely I thought the front bumper had touched on both sides.

'Want you to hold on to it,' he said. 'Not my money to carry.' He leaned my way, putting his elbow on the armrest between us. 'Things go bad, we lose it, *you* explain to your uncle.'

It took a moment for that to sink in. I could not believe my good luck: he was actually taking me to the exchange. Among all the possibilities I had considered, this was by far the best. I would not even have to open the bag, much less wait to see if he would count the short money that was in it. I would go to the exchange, wait for Skinny to arrive with his *troops*, give him the money myself.

'It not my deal,' DeLloyd added pointedly, glancing at me.

Ahead of us a truck had stopped and was starting to back up, angling into a loading bay. DeLloyd did not speed up, but he did not slow down, either.

'Aren't you going to—' I began, too late.

At the last possible moment he moved the wheel, jerking it back and forth, and again we slipped past, unscratched.

'Slow down,' I finished, relieved, then angry at the chances that he was taking. 'Do you always drive like this?' I asked sourly.

'Maybe,' he replied. 'Maybe just drive close when there somebody behind me.'

Startled, I turned to look, but he stopped me, one hand on my arm.

'Not cool to look,' he said. He was still leaning toward me, casually extended, one hand on top of the wheel. We came to an open stretch of street, and he glanced in the mirror, not accelerating but waiting, it seemed, for a car to catch up. 'Six years me and Lips parked cars at the Monteleone garage,' he began, enunciating the hotel's name strangely, derisively, making it two separate words. 'Sometimes, before we parked 'em, we took the cars out, the fine ones, made the block, thought we cool, played tag.' He smiled vaguely, to himself, then glanced in the mirror again. 'But Lips careless. Too wild. Can't drive as good as he think he can. He wrecked one, lost his job—lucky he didn't do time.' DeLloyd shifted in his seat, sitting up straight putting both hands on the wheel. 'I stop to tell you come down, go by the garage, he there, waiting. I tag his bumper. He it. Been tryin' to catch me ever since.'

'You're playing tag?' I asked, incredulous.

'Not hardly playing now, my friend,' he replied, a dark look crossing his face. 'We got scores to settle, me and him. This just warming us up.'

DeLloyd spun the wheel to the left in a turn so tight it bounced my head against the window. My stomach lurched.

'Lips wild,' he went on. 'Got a short temper. Make him mad, he forget himself, forget his plans.' He was driving hard now, working at it, cutting in and out of the slow-moving traffic. 'Shit go funny, you stay with me.'

'Shit go funny,' I repeated drily, 'you can count on it.'

DeLloyd was tense, concentrating, and for a while we did not speak. After a few blocks of watching closely I began to catch the rhythm of his driving. I saw that, despite the extraordinarily close tolerances of his maneuvers, he was not at all careless. Six years parking cars had left him with an uncanny ability to anticipate, to know both what his car and what the other cars around him would do. From the way his eyes flicked back and forth to the mirror, I knew Lips was just behind us, keeping up.

'Does Lips have the drugs in his car?' I

asked.

'Nigger's not too sharp,' DeLloyd replied, cursing softly as we skidded and one wheel bounced on the curb, 'but even he ain't dumb enough to keep the drugs in his car. Probably left 'em in the garage—that where we headed now.'

Thirty feet in front of us a woman stepped out into the street; heedless, not looking, she just walked straight ahead as she fooled with her umbrella, holding it up high, in front of her face. DeLloyd hit the brakes, hard, and we skidded badly, sliding sideways, stopping just short of her, alongside her, so close DeLloyd could have reached out and grabbed her. Out of the corner of my eye I saw motion on my side. I looked back in time to see the car that had been behind us coming right at me, its big chrome grille centered on my door.

I just watched it, frozen, its long, flat hood and its chrome hood ornament, sliding.

The car stopped, inches away, then moved forward and bumped us sharply.

'Shit,' DeLloyd swore, accelerating viciously, spinning the wheel, going around the woman and into a turn. 'That was Lips.' He swore again. 'We it.'

That's fucking nice, I thought, fear quickly transformed to anger, glancing back, seeing that the car that had tapped us was following but staying well back, not coming up—and seeing, too, across the back seat, a short, black, pump-action shotgun, sawed off, the kind the guards in the jail's towers used, clearing them at the end of each shift, staring us down if we looked up from the yard.

DeLloyd drove more slowly now, deliberately, drawn into himself, and, it appeared, very angry.

We were only two blocks from the garage, and I began to look for Skinny, knowing that he and his troops were likely well hidden, but looking just the same.

DeLloyd turned right, then right again, before he turned into the garage, not stopping, going past the shiny, expensive cars kept parked near the front, past the cashier's booth and the gas pumps, stopping only after he had pulled onto the large, square car-elevator; then he got out himself and closed the wire mesh gates, pressed a button, and started us up.

The elevator was closd only at the corners and across the gate—the sides and the top were open—and I caught a glimpse of Lips's car. I heard the roar of its laboring engine and its tires squealing, the sounds echoing hollowly, eerily, from the steep concrete ramp that spiraled up all around us.

I cursed for no particular reason, softly, to myself.

Between two parking levels DeLloyd pressed the button again. We stopped, and above us a black man appeared, lying flat on the floor, just his head and his hand stuck over the edge of the shaft.

'What's happening, my friend?' DeLloyd asked quietly.

'Lips just started up,' the man whispered back. 'He got one blood in the car with him; one more up top, in the office.' The man glanced at me, then back at DeLloyd. 'That all you brought with you?'

'Don't need no more, not for Lips,' he said, and started us up again.

'They got guns,' the man added.

DeLloyd said in a low whisper, 'You stay near the lights, like I told you.'

The squealing tires stopped, somewhere up high.

The elevator motor hummed quietly, a low, whining pulse.

Where is Skinny? I wondered. I clutched the brown paper bag very tightly. *What if he isn't here?*

Big trouble, I thought, making light of my anxiety, but I could feel my heart in my chest, a low, muffled pounding.

I glimpsed the rows of neatly parked cars as we passed; they were all very pale, colorless in the dim fluorescent light, and there was no one around them at all, not a person in sight.

The elevator stopped with a jolt.

DeLloyd looked around coolly, his nostrils flared wide, then opened the wire mesh gates.

Directly in front of us, between two huge concrete columns, a single parking space had been roped off with bright yellow rope and furnished with chairs, a low table, and a couch. It took me a moment to realize that that was the lounge, the *office* the man had mentioned, and not some bizarre, freestanding display. A soft-drink vending machine, its door cracked open, was wired into the large car battery that sat beside it, and there was a lamp near one end of the couch. The lamp was bent, its shade tilted rakishly, and in the harsh yellow light it cast was Lips, sitting back on the couch very nonchalantly, posed, his legs stretched out on the low wooden table, one arm draped over the back of the couch. He looked very different than he had when I had seen him in Skinny's trunk, taller and much more muscular. His eyes took in the car and me, then locked on DeLloyd in a flat, malevolent stare.

'Brother,' he said, the word drawn out to a hiss.

'I ain't your brother,' DeLloyd replied, his voice very low.

'Used to be—' Lips began.

'Used to be don't count for shit.' DeLloyd cut him off.

Lips did not move, but a tension went through him.

'Used to be,' he repeated very slowly,

'before you started turning too white.'

I thought for sure Lips had cut it, that he had gone too far with that slur—an impression that Lips apparently shared because when DeLloyd stepped forward, drawing himself up to his full impressive height, he reached quickly behind the couch, groping, it was obvious, for some weapon; but DeLloyd just asked, 'You got the drugs?' and stayed where he was.

'You got the money?' Lips snapped in reply, a hard challenge. He brought his arm back just a bit.

'He do,' DeLloyd said, jerking his head to one side, back at me.

Lip's black eyes slowly came my way again. I could see that he was weighing it, bouncing it back and forth, figuring whether or not he could mention Skinny without involving himself.

'Tell him get out the car,' he said to DeLloyd, though his eyes remained fixed on me.

I did not wait for DeLloyd to relay his order but pushed open the door, starting to get out, seeing too late DeLloyd shake his head, 'No,' as the door slammed back on my leg, once, then again. My breath expelled in a grunt. I tried to fall back, but a hand grabbed my hair, twisted my head, yanked me out of the car. The bag was stripped from my hand.

I heard a hard thud, a grunt not my own,

flesh smacked very sharply against flesh.

My crushed leg collapsed, and I fell, hitting the floor very hard, rolling, then seeing a man scrambling away, down low, crablike, moving back, away from DeLloyd.

'I just followin' orders,' the man protested. 'Ain't got no quarrel with you.'

'They not *my* orders, my friend,' DeLloyd said to him, then stepped forward and picked up the bag from the floor where it had dropped.

I must watch this very closely, I thought, feeling the press of the concrete beneath me more than the pain in my leg, *because it is the last small scene I will see.*

DeLloyd held the bag in his hands just a moment, then tossed it to Lips, flipping it backhand in a long, high arc to the couch.

Very slowly Lips sat forward, his eyes never leaving DeLloyd.

'Where's the drugs?' DeLloyd asked very roughly.

Lips did not reply right away but looked at the bag, then picked it up, feeling its good solid weight.

'Ain't no drugs,' he said, and smiled very coldly, leaning back on the couch again, reaching behind it, coming out with a gun. 'Never was none. I just taking your white man's money, *my friend*—going to leave you to explain.'

I could smell the concrete beneath my

cheek and the grease and the dirt that were on it.

'You takin' my money,' DeLloyd asked, 'and there ain't no Tees-and-Blues?'

I could not see his face, but his tone was deliberate and thoughtful.

'Ain't your money,' Lips snapped. 'It the white man's money.'

Lips got to his feet and stepped over the low table in front of him.

I closed my eyes, then opened them, seeing when I did the white ribs in Lips's socks and the shiny white surface on his loafers.

'You got the Tees, DeLloyd,' Lips went on, his expression a mocking sneer. 'They in your storehouse—get a cold, they good for what ails you. You just ain't got the Blues to go with them.' He shook the bag in his hand. 'Ain't got no Blues and ain't got no money, neither.'

For a long moment DeLloyd said nothing; what he did next surprised me: he stepped over to me and bent down, lifted my leg from the floor, and examined it gently, feeling the bone the length of my shin.

'You still *it*, too, brother,' Lips said to his back. 'Look like it not your lucky day.'

DeLloyd put my leg down as gently as he had lifted it.

'Your leg's not broke,' he said.

At the edge of my vision I saw motion, a figure moving between cars; then I saw

Skinny stand up straight, his silver revolver held out at arm's length.

'Freeze right there, you sorry bastard,' he yelled at Lips.

The revolver caught the light and reflected it, flashing.

Lips started and stopped, flinching.

DeLloyd swore softly.

Behind Lips, from behind a fat concrete column, another man appeared, holding a rifle, aiming it past Lips, back at Skinny.

Lips put his feet apart, shifting his weight, looked over his shoulder, then back, a smug smile playing across his face.

'Look like we at a stand-off,' he said very coolly.

The silver revolver did not waver. It remained fixed on Lips, pointed right at him.

'You think you can fuck with Skinny?' he said. His eyes were fierce and angry. 'Think again, asshole. You'll go first.' His chin jerked just slightly toward the man with the rifle. 'Call him off,' he said. 'Skinny hasn't got all night.'

Lips narrowed his eyes and cocked his head to one side, looking at Skinny with undisguised hate.

'I ain't going to jail,' he said flatly.

I felt DeLloyd's hand on the small of my back, pressing down hard, then he surprised me again: he whistled loudly, a hard, piercing blast of shrill sound that echoed hollowly, reverberating from the concrete all around us.

The lights began to blink out, one after another; but Skinny and Lips just stood where they were, eyes locked, neither moving. The last light flickered, dimming before it went out completely.

In the darkness that followed, the first shots came from the left, a short burst of rapid fire, and from the right a single concussing boom replied, a long straight flash of fire.

I felt myself lifted and dragged, pulled back onto the car-elevator; then thrown into DeLloyd's car, across the back seat. DeLloyd slid the shotgun out from under me.

I twisted on the seat, reaching into my pocket, taking out the small pistol that Stacey had given me, feeling how small it was, how unsubstantial.

When the next burst of gunfire came, DeLloyd got into his car and started it, keeping it at idle, running quietly as he waited for his eyes to adjust to the dark.

'One man ain't got the drugs,' he said out loud, to himself, his voice low and taut, angry. 'Other man ain't got the money. Shit.' He put the car in gear. 'What kind of a motherfuckin' deal you call that?' He racked the shotgun purposefully, slamming the heavy steel bolt open and closed, chambering a round, and laid it across his lap.

I sat up on the seat, trying to see in the

darkness.

How does he know that, I wondered suddenly, about the short-money? Only Stacey and I knew . . .

Stacey had to have called him, I thought, realizing in a rush what that could mean, allowing myself to hope before I was thrown back in the seat, flailing, trying to regain my balance as the car jumped forward full-throttle, out of the elevator, tires screaming onto the concrete in a smoking, blind turn.

As soon as the car straightened out DeLloyd switched on the headlights, in time to see that we were already entering the ramp, going too fast. He braked hard, but the car slid into the high curb. There was an abrupt jerk as the left front tire hit the cement. The rear end slid around, and there was a heavy thud as the left rear wheel slammed into the curb. Sheet metal ripped. I felt the impact in my teeth. DeLloyd turned the wheel hard to the right and spun the car off the curb, bringing it to a shuddering stop before he shifted down and accelerated again, going down the ramp, down in tight circles, the tires squealing continuously until we saw bright flashing lights coming up, throwing long shadows that blinked, and he stopped very quickly and put the car out of gear.

'Get out,' he said. 'Get out and hold your hands where the policemen can see 'em.'

He threw open the passenger-side door before he got out himself.

The trembling seemed to start in my hands and my knees, waves of quaking fear, too long suppressed, that ran uncontrollably through me.

DeLloyd whistled again.

I shut my eyes as the lights came back on, dimly at first, then brighter.

* * *

The policemen put DeLloyd and me in the backseats of two different cars, then they sped back up the ramp and parked, one behind the other on the last short stretch of incline, in close to the curb. They ran off very quickly, leaving us there, then after a few minutes one of them returned to turn off the cars, and a few minutes after that an ambulance arrived, lights flashing, squeezing past on the left. I could not see what was happening so I laid my head back on the seat and waited, not thinking, listening to the police radio squawk softly in code. Once or twice I shifted position, trying to ease the throbbing pain in my leg.

The ambulance left very slowly, without the flashing urgency that had marked its arrival, and as it squeezed past again I saw Skinny behind it, walking slowly, both hands in his jacket pockets, head down. When he saw that I was watching him, he looked back up the ramp, took one hand out of his pocket, ran that hand over his face. Reluctantly, it seemed, he came over to the car in which I was sitting, opened the door, and got in beside me. He reached into his pocket, came out with a scrap of paper.

'Skinny thought he had 'em, Curbel,' he said. He spit out the piece of gum he had had in his mouth, wrapped the scrap of paper around it. 'He thought they were all going down.'

I did not reply to him but kept my eyes to the front.

He tossed the paper-wrapped wad of gum out the door and allowed his eyes to follow it.

'Lips never called,' Skinny went on, still looking out the door. 'He never called Skinny to tell him about the deal because he knew there wasn't going to be a deal. There never were any drugs.'

Skinny shook his head from side to side, glanced at me, then away.

'When Skinny first caught up to Lips, in the projects, he asked Lips's momma where he got that name, Lips.' He shook his head again. 'Lips,' he repeated. 'His momma said she had started calling him that when he was a boy because he was always talking, giving her lip.'

Skinny took out a fresh piece of gum, began to unwrap it, reconsidered, and put it back in his pocket. He turned to face me, putting one arm along the back of the seat and drawing one leg up between us.

'The Tees-and-Blues were just talk, Curbel—at least that's the way Skinny figures it. Lips was just shooting off his mouth about having the drugs, but your little honey, Veldran, she didn't know that. She set Lips up on the rape charge to force him to deal, but surprise: the only drugs he could get he had to buy at the pharmacy. So Lips probably figured, what the shit? If his story was good enough to get him into jail, it was good enough to get him out again, too—with a little work, he could even make some money from it.' Skinny raised and dropped both shoulders at once. 'And we all bought it. Even Skinny.'

Even Skinny, I thought, picturing Lips in the trunk of Skinny's car, laughing to himself in the darkness as he ate the raw ears of corn.

'The poor bastard was jammed from the start,' Skinny said.

The radio sounded a loud, beeping tone, and Skinny's eyes flicked toward the sound, then back to me.

'Whose money is that in the bag?' he asked. 'Yours?'

I nodded cautiously, allowing that it was.

'That's what Skinny figured, too,' he went on quickly. 'Whether or not it's yours, you'd claim it, right? You'd say you were working for Skinny, just doing what you were told, making a buy, so you'd cut off the connection back to your family?'

It was not really a question the way he said it; it was more a suggestion or an order—and that puzzled me. I pretended not to have noticed his tone.

'I have the agency's books,' I said. 'They don't show much, I'm afraid.'

'There weren't any drugs, Curbel,' Skinny replied tiredly, too readily dismissing the books. 'They don't show anything at all.'

I thought about that for a moment, only beginning to realize what he was doing: for some reason, it seemed Skinny, too, wanted to hide the other connections.

'But you're in the clear with Skinny,' he added, 'if that's what you meant.'

That was way too easy.

'I'm not going back to jail?' I asked very tentatively, expecting a hook, some outrageous condition.

'Nah,' he replied, stretching his mouth very wide. 'What fun would that be? Skinny wants you out for now. He wants to see what you'll get into next—there's always a next time, right? Skinny'll be here, Curbel. He can wait.' He smiled in a menacingly good-humored way, his lips sliding off his protruding front teeth, then in one quick motion he got out of the car and in again, in front, behind the wheel.

'You ever ride in a police car before?' he asked as he started the motor. 'Sure you have,' he answered himself, and abruptly threw the car into gear.

I did not understand what he was doing, why he appeared to be backing off so completely, but I just sat quietly as he drove up the ramp and stopped in front of the car-elevator, just across from the lounge.

A policeman in uniform approached the car, but Skinny waved him away, then turned back to me, looking at me curiously over the back of the seat.

'There's just one thing that Skinny can't figure, Curbel,' he said. 'Maybe you can set him straight.' He ducked his head forward to run his hand through his hair, front to back. 'Skinny can't understand why you'd do somebody else's time and just let it go. For what, Curbel? What's in it for you?'

I pressed my lips together and shook my head from side to side, knowing that, even if I wanted to, I could not explain it to him because I could just barely explain it to myself.

'You're just being a nice guy, right?' he went on when he saw I was not going to answer. He slid across the seat, opened the passenger-side door, got out, and opened my door, pulling it wide and holding it there, standing in front of it. 'So, Curbel,' he said, and stepped out of the way, opening my view.

'You want to say good-bye to Lips?'

I watched him. I watched those shrewd, feral eyes mocking me until he looked away, coyly, half-amused.

A few feet away, Lips was just where I had seen him last, where he had been standing when the lights had gone out; but now he was lying on the concrete in a large pool of blood, one leg outstretched, the other twisted beneath him grotesquely. His purple-black eyes were wide open, staring unseeing. More blood ran out of his ear.

'His own man got him,' Skinny said, and jerked a thumb to the left, 'the guy who popped out with a rifle—zipped him right up the back.'

A tremor ran through Lips's outstretched leg, a twitching, convulsive spasm that threw off his white loafer, exposing a hole in the heel of his thin, white-ribbed sock.

'The rattles,' Skinny said. 'Spooky, huh? Skinny'll check with the coroner, see how long it'll be before they scrape him up.'

I watched Skinny walk away, stepping around the body and the blood, then, as if on their own, my eyes went back to Lips, seeing the surprise on his face, and the pain.

'Looks like it not your lucky day,' he had said to DeLloyd.

'The poor bastard was jammed from the start,' Skinny had said about him.

At least you won't have to go back to jail, I

thought.

I felt a great sadness well up in me, a deep sense of regret.

Across the way Skinny sat down on the couch and put one boot up on the low table as he spoke animatedly, gesturing into the portable radio he had borrowed from the policeman who stood nearby.

When had this really begun, I wondered. When had the stage been set? When Ellis had seduced his nurse, Stacey's mother? When Lips had begun to tell stories? Or did it go back even further than that, to when that first Curbelo had claimed Mochita as his own and somehow convinced his son that he had to keep it? What right did he have, I wondered, to lay that off on all those who followed? How many people had died?

'You will do what you have to do,' my own father had told me. 'You are a Curbel.'

I tried to muster anger or outrage, but my emotions seemed all used up. I looked again at Lips, then past him to Skinny, who was eyeing me coolly, tapping the radio's short antenna thoughtfully against his chin.

Skinny, too, was at fault. I could see that now, more immediately. Skinny had known that Lips had been set up by Stacey, but he had allowed the false charge to stand. For whatever his reasons, good or bad, he had wanted his bust too badly. He had encouraged the deal, trying to get at my family, and the one real victim lay dead as a result, still twitching. It followed, then, that he wanted to hide the connections, to make it appear simply that a deal had gone bad. I was surprised I had not seen it sooner.

Skinny smiled conspiratorially, as if he had just read my thoughts.

Very deliberately I got out of the car, pulling myself out on my good leg, gingerly testing the other. For a long moment I looked very closely at Lips.

'Leave, Curbel,' Skinny called out to me, 'and take your buddy with you.' He jerked his head to the left, toward the ramp and the car in which DeLloyd was sitting. He smiled again, a smile that did not touch his eyes. 'Skinny'll catch up to you later.'

CHAPTER SIXTEEN

DeLloyd drove slowly, sedately, going out of the French Quarter, passing my newsdealer's now empty stand, turning onto Canal Street and heading out toward the lake. Just as I had opened the door to the police car to let him out, the coroner's van had come up the ramp, and I had had to close the door again to let it pass. 'Lips?' DeLloyd had asked before he had gotten out. 'Yes,' I had replied firmly, and since then we had not spoken at all; both of us were turned inward, occupied with our own thoughts.

DeLloyd stopped at a grocery and went inside, returning a few minutes later with a large bag of ice, a big roll of gray tape, and a pocket-sized bottle of Scotch. Without a word, he opened my door, took my leg very gently, put the whole bag of ice on my shin, and taped it there, wrapping the tape over the bag and over my pants; then he squatted down on his heels, opened the Scotch, took a quick swallow, and handed the bottle to me.

I took a long swallow and started to hand back the bottle, but he waved it away.

'I talk to Stacey just now,' he said. 'Called her.' He waved one hand at the grocery. 'She say Esperoza got back his two boys.'

I started to ask, 'Where did she have them hidden?' but thought better of it, and asked instead, 'When did she tell you I didn't have all the money?'

DeLloyd's dark glance held impatience.

'She say Esperoza promised to turn loose your father—maybe already has.'

I nodded, not surprised but relieved—and grateful.

DeLloyd's eyes slipped away, to the rear window, then back.

'Stacey called me just before I picked you up at your apartment, told me about the short-money.' His eyes slipped away again. 'She say there wasn't enough there to get hurt over. She say we ought just to let it go and forget it.'

Let it go and forget it, I thought, leaning back in the seat, thinking of Stacey, of the decision that she had made. By trying to call off the deal she was herself trying to do just what she had advised DeLloyd, trying to let go of what was past and forget it. I felt pleased for her, but I thought, too, of the events she had put in motion, of the damage that had been done.

'But you can't just let it go,' DeLloyd went on, 'not just like that, not when it so close.' DeLloyd turned his face away from me. 'Can't believe Lips didn't have no drugs. Can't let him go with nothing. I knew that boy—should have known. Should have just let it go like she said.'

'Let it go now,' I said, seeing that DeLloyd's broad shoulders were bowed, knowing what I had planned for him and feeling a powerful guilt course through me. 'Lips ran his own game. He knew the risk.'

'Your uncle, he needed—' DeLloyd began, then stopped himself abruptly. He ran one big hand over his face.

'I guess I'll go to see your uncle,' he said. 'Make sure that old man is okay.'

'Ellis is all right,' I assured him. 'He's too ornery to be down for long.'

DeLloyd pushed himself to his feet.

'Where you want to go?' he asked.

I thought about that only for a moment. 'Take me to my father's house,' I said.

* * *

As DeLloyd drove to the end of Canal Street and turned left, going past the cemeteries before crossing the parish line, we did not speak. A silence settled between us that neither of us seemed to know how to break. I put the top back on the bottle of Scotch and after a while just looked out the window.

As we neared my father's house I noted the familiar landmarks—the cleaner's, the shoe repair shop, the service station that had been there for years—and a familiar tension overtook that awkward silence, a foreboding that mixed with dread.

I did not know what I would say to my father when I saw him—or what I expected him to say to me. So many things had changed in the year since I had seen him; so many events had taken place in the last few hours. At best, even when we had the everyday in common, there was a vast distance between my father and me, a great difference in outlook, priorities, and temperament. Yet I knew there was, too, in all the days we had shared and survived, the mainstay of my history. My father had always been there for me, the solid rock upon which I had built. From the events of his life alone, it was easy to understand the insecurity that drove him and the need to dominate that had resulted, his need to feel that he was in charge; but that understanding still did not make it easy to endure his withering appraisals of me and whatever I did, the doubt he created inside me.

DeLloyd started to turn into the driveway, changed his mind, pulled up alongside the curb. He got out, went around the car, held my door wide to help me get out. When he offered his hand, I took it.

I stood up, and cold water dripped into my shoe. I kicked the shoe off, looked up, and saw that DeLloyd was just standing there, watching me; for one long moment our eyes locked, and in that glance something strong passed between us, some feeling I did not understand right away.

DeLloyd nodded once, got into his car, pulled into the driveway to turn around. I sat down on the curb to remove the ice from my leg. As I unwound the layers of tape, pulling it slowly at first, then faster, I heard him go past and saw him put on his blinker, preparing to turn, then turning, going back the way we had come.

I wadded the tape into a sticky ball and rolled it in one hand, squeezing it tightly. The street was very quiet and dark, and sitting there on the curb I patted my pockets for my keys, then took a few minutes to study the house before I went in, observing again the small, square windows, the steeply pitched roof, the precisely cut grass. It had been well over a year since I had visited, yet suddenly it seemed no time at all had passed. Nothing had changed.

An overhead light came on in the middle window, near the desk lamp that was always left on, and I knew exactly what that meant: my father was at home, already released, already there in his study, starting to open his mail.

I felt a sense of relief and something else that ran deeper.

A shadow moved near the desk, and I knew he was picking out the bills and letters he thought were important and sorting through the rest very quickly, putting most of it straight into the trash. And just as I knew his expression right then and the exact way that he was standing—slouched just a bit, head cocked to one side, the corners of his mouth turned down in dour concentration—I knew how he would look when he opened the door, how the surprise would register when he saw me.

Behind the lighted window the shadow moved again, and I knew what that meant too: he was going to his file cabinet taking out his large, black checkbook, preparing to write checks for his bills.

In me a certain space of time seemed

bridged; my memories seemed more like echoes, reflections direct from a living source, not something dead in the past.

I stood up from the curb, brushed off the seat of my pants, threw the sticky ball of tape at a culvert. I straightened my jacket and smoothed down my hair before I crossed the street and went up the walk, up to my father's front door.

Photoset, printed and bound in Great Britain by REDWOOD PRESS LIMITED, Melksham, Wiltshire